CLAUDINE AND ANNIE

Colette had a long, varied, and active life. Her childhood in the Burgundian village of Saint-Sauveur-en-Puisaye, where she was born in 1873 and afterwards educated at the local school, was a period of deep happiness. At the age of twenty she was plunged into a different world by her marriage to the notorious 'Willy'. The marriage was an unhappy one, though Colette learnt much from it. She left her husband, and spent six years on the music-hall stage. Later, she worked as special correspondent and theatre critic – writing books all the time. She divorced her second husband (by whom she had one daughter), and in 1935 married M. Goudeket with whom she lived in Paris until her death in 1954. During her last years she was crippled with arthritis, but her zest for life was undiminished. Her collected works – of which the best-known are probably the novels *La Maison de Claudine* (1922) and *Sido* (1929) – run to fifteen volumes. She was elected to the Académie Goncourt in 1936.

COLETTE

CLAUDINE AND ANNIE

Translated by Antonia White

PENGUIN BOOKS
in association with Secker & Warburg

Penguin Books Ltd, Harmondsworth, Middlesex, England
Penguin Books Australia Ltd, Ringwood, Victoria, Australia

—

Claudine s'en va first published 1903
This translation published by Secker & Warburg 1962
Published in Penguin Books 1963
Reissued 1972

—

—

Made and printed in Great Britain
by C. Nicholls & Company Ltd
Set in Linotype Pilgrim

ONE

HE has gone! He has gone! I keep saying those words to myself; now I am writing them down on paper to find out if they are true and if they are going to hurt me. As long as he was there, I did not feel as if he were going. He bustled about methodically. He kept giving precise orders and insisting: 'Annie, be sure not to forget . . .' then breaking off to say: 'Goodness, how miserable you look! Your distress distresses me more than the prospect of going away!' Did I really look so miserable? I was not suffering, because he was still there.

Hearing him pity me like that made me shiver inwardly. Shrunk into myself, I kept wondering fearfully: 'Am I really going to be as unhappy as he says? This is terrible.'

At the moment it is all too true. He has gone! I am afraid to move, to breathe, to live. A husband ought not to leave his wife – not when it is this particular husband and this particular wife.

Before I had turned thirteen, he was already the master of my life. Such a handsome master! A red-haired boy, with a skin whiter than an egg and blue eyes that dazzled me. When I lived with my grandmother Lajarrisse – she was all the family I had – I used to look forward and count the days to his summer holidays. At last the morning would arrive when she would come into my nunlike little grey and white bedroom (they whitewash the walls down there because of the fierce summer heat and they stay fresh and clean in the shadow of the shutters) and say, as she entered: 'Alain's bedroom windows are open, cook saw them when she came back from town.' She would announce this calmly without suspecting that those mere words made me curl up into a tight little ball under my sheets and draw my knees up to my chin ...

Alain! At twelve years old I loved him, as I do now, with a confused, frightened love that had no trace of coquetry or guile in it. Every year we were inseparable companions for close on four months because he was being educated in Normandy at one of those schools modelled on English lines where the boys have long summer holidays. He would arrive all white and golden, with five or six freckles under his blue eyes, and push open the garden gate as if he were planting a flag on a conquered citadel. I used to wait for him in my little everyday frock ... not daring to dress up for him in case he noticed it. He would take me off with him and we would read or play. He never asked for my opinion; he jeered at me a good deal; he issued decrees. 'This is what we're going to do. You're to hold the foot of the ladder and stretch out your pinafore so that I can throw the apples into it.' He would put his arm round my shoulders and look about him menacingly as if to say: 'I dare anyone to take her from me!' He was sixteen and I was twelve.

Sometimes – I made that gesture again, humbly, only yesterday – I would lay my sunburnt hand on his white wrist and sigh: 'How black I am!' He would give a proud smile that displayed his square teeth and reply: '*Sed formosa*, Annie dear.'

I have a photograph here, taken in those days. I am dark and slight, as I am now, with a small head dragged back a little by the heavy black hair and a pouting mouth that seems to be pleading 'I won't do it again'. Under the very long lashes that grow in one dense perfectly straight sweep, the eyes are of such a liquid blue that they embarrass me when I look at myself in the glass – they are

6

so ridiculously light against a skin as dark as a little Kabyle girl's. However, since Alain found them attractive . . .

We grew up very virtuously, without any kissing or erotic behaviour. That was not due to me! I would have said 'Yes' without even uttering a word. Sometimes, when I was with him towards evening, I found the scent of jasmine too oppressive and my throat felt so constricted I could hardly breathe . . . Since words failed me to tell Alain: 'This jasmine, this twilight, this down on my own skin that caresses my lips when they brush it . . . they're all you . . .' I would press my lips together and lower my lashes over my too-light eyes in an attitude so habitual to me that he never once suspected anything . . . He is as upright and decent as he is handsome.

At twenty-four, he announced: 'Now we're going to get married' just as eleven years earlier he would have announced: 'Now we're going to play Indians.'

He has always known so infallibly what I ought to do that without him I am lost. I am like a useless mechanical toy that has lost its key. How am I to know now what is right and what is wrong?

Poor weak, selfish little Annie! Thinking of him makes me feel sorry for myself. I implored him not to go away . . . I said very little because his affection, always reserved, dreads emotional outbursts. 'Perhaps this legacy doesn't amount to much . . . We've got enough money as it is, and it's a long way to go on the off-chance of finding a fortune . . . Alain, suppose you commissioned someone else . . .' His astonished eye-brows cut me short in the middle of my tactless suggestion, but I plucked up courage again. 'Well then, Alain, couldn't you take me with you?'

His pitying smile deprived me of all hope.

'Take you with me, my poor child? You . . . delicate

as you are ... and ... I don't want to hurt your feelings ... such a bad traveller? Can you see yourself enduring the voyage to Buenos Aires? Think of your health, think ... and I know this is an argument that will convince you ...'of the trouble you might be to *me*.' I lowered my lids, which is my way of retiring into my shell, and silently cursed my Uncle Etchevarray, a hothead who disappeared fifteen years ago and of whom we had heard nothing till now. Tiresome idiot, why did he take it into his head to die rich in some unknown country and leave us ... what? ... Some *estancias* where they breed bulls, 'bulls that sell at up to six thousand piastres, Annie'. I can't even remember what that adds up to in francs.

The day of his departure is not over yet and here I am in my room, secretly writing in the beautiful notebook he gave me for the purpose of keeping my 'Diary of his journey'. I am also re-reading the list of duties he drew up for me with his usual solicitous firmness. It is headed *Timetable*.

June. Calls on Madame X—, Madame Z—, and Madame T— (important).

Only one call on Renaud and Claudine. Too fantastically unconventional a couple for a young woman to frequent while her husband is away on a long journey.

Pay the upholsterer's bill for the big armchairs in the drawing-room and the cane bedstead. Don't haggle because the upholsterer works for our friends the G.s. People might gossip.

Order Annie's summer clothes. Not too many 'tailored' things; light, simple dresses. Will my dear Annie not obstinately persist in believing that red and bright orange make her complexion look lighter?

8

Check the servants' account books every Saturday morning. See that Jules does not forget to take down the tapestry in my smoking-room and that he rolls it up sprinkled with pepper and tobacco. He's not a bad fellow but slack and he'll do his jobs carelessly if Annie doesn't keep a sharp eye on him.

Annie will take a daily walk in the Avenues and will not read too much nonsense. Not too many 'realistic' novels or any other kind.

Warn the 'Urbaine' that we are giving notice on July 1st. Hire the Victoria by the day during the five days before you go off to Arriège.

My dear Annie will give me much pleasure if she frequently consults my sister Marthe and goes out with her. Marthe has a great deal of good sense and even common sense under her rather unconventional exterior.

He has thought of everything! Don't I have, even for one minute, any shame about my . . . my incompetence? Inertia would be a better word perhaps . . . or passivity. Alain's active vigilance overlooks nothing and spares me from the slightest practical worry. By nature I am as indolent as a little Negress but, in the first year of our marriage, I did attempt to shake myself out of my silent languor. Alain made short work of destroying my noble zeal. 'Leave it alone, Annie, the thing's done. I've seen to it myself.' 'No, no, Annie, you don't know, you haven't the remotest idea . . . .!'

I don't know anything . . . except how to obey. He has taught me that and I achieve obedience as the sole task of my existence . . . assiduously . . . joyfully. My supple neck, my dangling arms, my too-slender, flexible shape . . . everything about me, from my eyelids that droop easily and say 'yes' to my little slave-girl's complexion, predestined me to obey. Alain often calls me

9

that, 'little slave-girl'. Of course he says it without malice, with only a faint contempt for my dark-skinned race. He is so white!

Yes, dear 'timetable', that will continue to guide me in his absence and until his first letter arrives, yes, I will give notice to the 'Urbaine'. I will keep an eye on Jules, I will check the servants' account books, I will pay my calls, and I will see Marthe frequently.

Marthe is my sister-in-law, Alain's sister. Although he disapproves of her having married a novelist, albeit a well-known one, my husband is aware of her lively, scatter-brained intelligence and her intermittent clear-sightedness. He readily admits: 'She's clever.' I am not quite sure how to assess the value of that compliment.

In any case, she knows infallibly how to handle her brother and I am sure Alain has not the least suspicion how she plays up to him. How artfully she glosses over the risky word she has allowed to slip out, how deftly she glances off from a dangerous topic of conversation! When I have annoyed my lord and master, I just remain completely miserable, without even pleading to be forgiven. Marthe just laughs in his face, or tactfully admires some remark he has just made or is amusingly scathing about some particularly odious bore – and Alain's scowling eyebrows relax.

Clever, certainly, at using her wits and her hands. I watch her in amazement when, all the time she is chattering, her fingers are busy creating an adorable hat or a lace jabot with the professional skill of a 'first hand' in a good fashion-house. All the same, there is nothing of the 'little milliner' about Marthe. She is dimpled and rather short, with a tight-laced, very slim waist, and a shapely, provocative behind. She carries her head of flaming red-gold hair (Alain's hair) very high, and she has glittering, ruthless grey eyes. Her face is the face of

a young incendiary – a fierce little female 'comrade' –
and she composes it into a charming pastiche of an
eighteenth-century court lady. She uses powder and
lipstick and wears rustling silk dresses patterned with
garlands of flowers, pointed bodices, and very high heels.
Claudine (the amusing Claudine whom one mustn't see
too much of) calls her 'The Marquise of the Barricades'.

This revolutionary Ninon de Lenclos has completely
subjugated the husband she conquered after a brief
struggle – there again I recognize her kinship with Alain:
Léon is rather like Marthe's Annie. When I think of him,
I mentally call him 'poor old Léon'. Nevertheless, he
does not look unhappy. He is dark, good-looking, with
regular features, a pointed beard, almond-shaped eyes
and soft hair plastered close to his skull. A typical Frenchman of the mild, unassertive kind. He would be more
impressive if his profile were a little more forceful, his
chin squarer, and his brows more emphatically drawn,
also if his brown eyes were not so eagerly anxious to
please. He is a trifle – it's malicious of me to write it –
a trifle 'head salesman in the silk department' as that
wicked Claudine suggested when she nicknamed him
one day: 'And-what-next-Madam?' The label has stuck
to poor old Léon whom Marthe treats merely as a pro-
ductive piece of property.

She shuts him up regularly for three or four hours
a day, with the result that he furnishes, she told me
confidentially, a good average yield of one and two-
thirds novels per year – 'enough for our bare necessities,'
she added.

It is beyond me that there should be women with
enough initiative and enough constant, persevering will
– enough cruelty too – to build up an income large
enough to sustain an extravagant way of life on the bent
back of a man who is forced to write and write till he

nearly kills himself. Sometimes I condemn Marthe; at others, she inspires me with admiration tinged with fear.

Thinking of her masculine authority that exploited Léon's meekness, I said to her one day, when I was feeling extraordinarily bold:

'Marthe, you and your husband are an unnatural couple.'

She stared at me in stupefaction, then she laughed till she nearly made herself ill.

'No, really ... the things our little Annie says! You ought never to go without a dictionary. An unnatural couple! Luckily, there's no one to hear you but me, considering what those words imply nowadays ...'

The fact remains that Alain has gone! I can't forget him for long while I run on like this, talking to myself on paper. What am I to do? This burden of living alone overwhelms me ... Suppose I go off to the country – to Casamène – to the house my grandmother Lajarrisse left us, so as to see no one, no one at all till he comes back?

Marthe came in at that point, sweeping away all my splendid, ridiculous plans with her stiff skirts and her rustling sleeves. Hurriedly, I hid my notebook.

'All by yourself? Are you coming to the tailor's? All alone in this dreary room? The inconsolable widow, in fact!'

Her ill-timed jest ... and also her likeness to her brother in spite of the powder, the Marie-Antoinette shepherdess hat and the tall parasol ... made me start crying again.

'There, now I've done it! Annie, you are the most abject of ... wives. He'll come back, I tell you! In my simple-minded, unworthy way, I imagined his absence

... anyway for the first few weeks ... would give you a holiday feeling – that it would actually be rather a lark ...'

'A lark ? Oh ! Marthe ...'

'Why, "Oh ! Marthe" ? ... I admit it feels empty here,' she said, wandering round the room, *my* room, where nothing, in fact, has changed.

I dried my eyes, which always takes a little time because I have such thick lashes. Marthe says, with a laugh, that I have 'hair on my eyelids'.

She turned her back to me and leant with both elbows on the mantelpiece. She was wearing – a little early for the time of the year, I thought – a high-waisted beige voile dress sprinkled with little old-fashioned roses, with a gathered skirt and a cross-over fichu in the style of Madame Vigée-Lebrun. Her red hair, swept up from the nape, was typical of a very different painter – Helleu. The two styles clashed a little, but not crudely. But I shall keep these remarks to myself. After all, what remarks do I *not* keep to myself ?

'What are you studying for such a long time, Marthe ?'

'I'm contemplating the portrait of his lordship, my brother.'

'Alain ?'

'Right first time.'

'What do you find so striking about him ?'

She did not answer at once. Then she burst out laughing and said, turning round :

'It's extraordinary how like a cock he is !'

'A cock ?'

'Yes, a cock. Just look.'

Horrified to hear such a blasphemy, I mechanically picked up the portrait, a photograph printed in reddish sepia. It's one I'm very fond of. My husband is standing, bare-headed, in a summer garden, with his red hair bristling, his eyes glaring haughtily, and his calves braced taut. That is his habitual stance. He looks like a robust, handsome young man with a fiery disposition and an alert eye; he also looks like a cock. Marthe was right. Yes a red, shiny-plumaged, crested and spurred cock ... As miserable as if he had just gone away all over again, I relapsed once more into tears. My sister-in-law threw up her arms in consternation.

'No, really, if one can't even mention him! You're a case, my dear. It's going to be a gay expedition to the tailor's with your eyes in that state! Have I hurt your feelings?'

'No, no, it's just *me* ... Take no notice, I'll be all right in a minute.'

The fact is that I couldn't admit to her that I was appalled that Alain should look like a cock and even more appalled that I should have realized it ... A cock! Why did she have to make me notice that?

TWO

'MADAME didn't sleep very well?'

'No, Léonie.'

'Madame has black rings round her eyes ... Madame should take a glass of brandy.'

Léonie knows only one remedy for all ills – a glass of brandy. I imagine she tests its good effects daily. She intimidates me a little because she is tall and very decisive in her movements. She has an authoritative way of shutting doors and when she is sewing in the linen-room she whistles military bugle-calls, like a coachman who has just returned from his regiment. Nevertheless she is capable of devotion and she has worked for me, ever since my marriage four years ago, with affectionate contempt.

That solitary awakening! There I was, all alone, telling myself that a day and a night had gone by since Alain left, summoning up all my courage to order meals, telephone to the 'Urbaine', go through the account books! ... A schoolboy who had not done his holiday task could not have woken up more depressed on the first morning of term ...

Yesterday, I did not accompany my sister-in-law to her fitting. I felt angry with her about that business of the cock. I pleaded tiredness and the redness of my eyelids.

Today I want to shake myself out of my nervous depression and – since Alain has ordered me to – go to Marthe's at-home day, though crossing that immense drawing-room, full of the babel of women's voices, alone and unsupported has always been a torture to me.

Suppose, as Claudine says, I 'reported sick'! Oh, no, I can't disobey my husband.

'Which dress does Madame want?'

Yes, which dress? Alain would not have hesitated for a moment. With one glance, he would have considered the state of the weather and of my complexion, then the names on Marthe's visiting-list and his impeccable choice would have satisfied every contingency...

'My grey crêpe dress, Léonie, and the hat with the butterflies.'

They amuse me, those grey butterflies with their soft feather wings speckled with pink and orange crescents. At least I must admit that my great sorrow hasn't had too disastrous an effect on my looks. With the butterfly hat set very straight on my smooth, thick hair, parted on the right and knotted in a low chignon, and my pale, disturbing blue eyes, more liquid than ever from recent tears, I could count on infuriating Valentine Chessenet. She is one of my sister-in-law's most faithful 'regulars' and she loathes me because (I can sense this) she finds my husband very much to her taste. That creature looks as if she had been dipped in a bleaching bath. Her hair, her skin, her eyelashes, are all of the same uniform pinkish fairness. She makes her face up pink and plasters her lashes with mascara (Marthe told me this herself) without managing to liven up her insipid, anaemic colouring.

She would already have taken up her post at Marthe's, with her back to the light to hide the bags under her eyes, as far away as possible from the lovely, stupid Cabbage-Rose whose healthy radiance she dreads. She would screech nasty things at me over the heads of the other women and I should be incapable of making any retort; my intimidated silence would make the other parakeets laugh and call me 'the little black goose' again. Alain, it is only for you that I am off to expose myself to all those painful pinpricks.

The moment I reached the hall, my hands went cold at the sound of that hen-house cackle, punctuated by the clatter of little spoons like the sound of pecking beaks.

Of course that Chessenet woman was there! They were all there and all chattering away, except Candeur, the child-poetess, whose silent soul only blossoms in beautiful verses. *She* kept quiet, slowly rolling her mottled eyes and biting her lower lips with a voluptuous, guilty air, as if it were someone else's.

There was Miss Flossie who, when she refuses a cup of tea, utters such a prolonged, guttural 'No' that she seems to be offering her whole self in that throaty purr. Alain (why?) does not want me to know her, that American woman, supple as a piece of silk, with her sparkling face glittering with tiny gold hairs, her sea-blue eyes, and her ruthless teeth. She smiled at me without a trace of embarrassment, her eyes riveted on mine, till a curious quiver of her left eyebrow, as disturbing as an appeal, made me look away ... At that, Miss Flossie gave me a more nervous smile while a slim, red-haired young girl huddled in her shadow glared at me with inexplicable hatred in her deep eyes.

Maugis – a fat music critic – his protruding eyes flashing for a second, stared straight at the two Americans so insolently that he deserved to be hit, and mumbled almost inaudibly as he filled a claret-glass with whisky:

'Some Sappho ... if that sort of thing amuses you!'

I didn't understand. I hardly dared look at all those faces suddenly fixed in a malicious rigidity because I was wearing a pretty frock. How I longed to escape! I took refuge by Marthe who revived me with her firm little hand and her audacious eyes, courageous as herself. How I envy her for being so brave. She has a sharp, impatient tongue, and she is very extravagant; she could easily be a target for unkind gossip. She is well aware of it and has a method of forestalling any spiteful innuendo : she gets her teeth into any treacherous female friend and shakes her with the tenacity of a good ratting terrier.

Today, I could have hugged her for her retort to Madame Chessenet who shrieked as I entered the room :

'Ah ! Here comes the Hindu widow !'

'Don't tease her too much,' Marthe flashed. 'After all, when a husband goes off, it leaves a void.'

A penetrating voice behind me, a voice that rolled its r's, acquiesced :

'Certainly . . . a verry considerrable and painful void !'

And all those women burst out laughing. I turned round in confusion and was more confused than ever when I saw that it was Renaud's wife, Claudine. 'Only one call on Renaud and Claudine, too fantastically unconventional a couple . . .' Alain treats them so distantly that I feel stupid and almost guilty in their presence. Nevertheless, I find them charming and to be envied, that husband and wife who never leave each other and are as united as lovers.

One day, when I was admitting to Alain that I didn't blame Claudine and Renaud in the least for posing as married lovers, he asked me rather sharply :

'My dear, where did you get the notion that lovers see each other and enjoy each other's company more than married people ?'

I replied sincerely :

'I've no idea . . .'

Ever since then, we have only exchanged occasional formal visits with this 'fantastic' couple.

This doesn't embarrass Claudine in the slightest, for nothing embarrasses her. Renaud doesn't mind either, for the only thing in the world he minds about is his wife. Yet Alain has a perfect horror of breaking with people unnecessarily.

Claudine seemed perfectly unaware that she had raised a laugh. She lowered her eyes and went on eating a lobster sandwich, announcing calmly when she had finished it: 'That's the sixth.'

'Yes,' said Marthe gaily, 'you're an expensive acquaintance. The soul of Madame Beulé has passed into you.'

'Only her stomach, the one thing she had worth taking,' Claudine corrected her.

'Take care, dear,' insinuated Madame Chessenet. 'You'll get fat on that diet. It struck me the other night that your arms were filling out into a charming but dangerous roundness.'

'Pooh!' retorted Claudine, with her mouth full. 'I only wish you had thighs as round as my arms. So many people would be pleased if you had.'

Madame Chessenet, who is skinny and bitterly laments it, swallowed this rebuff with difficulty. Her neck was so tense that I feared there was going to be a little scene. However she merely glared in mute fury at the insolent young woman with the short hair and rose to her feet. I was on the point of getting up to go myself, but I sat down again so as not to have to leave the room with that bleached viper.

Claudine valiantly attacked the plate of little cream cakes topped with praline and offered me one (if Alain had seen us! . . .). I accepted, and whispered to her:

'That Chessenet woman's going to invent most appalling scandals about you!'

'I defy her to. She's already brought out everything she's capable of imagining. There's nothing she hasn't attributed to me except infanticide and I wouldn't even be too sure of that.'

'She doesn't like you ?' I asked her shyly.

'Oh yes, she does. But she conceals the fact.'

'Don't you mind ?'

'Of course I do.'

'Why ?'

Claudine's beautiful tobacco-brown eyes stared at me.

'Why ? *I* don't know. Because . . .'

Her husband's approach broke off her reply. Smiling, he unobtrusively pointed towards the door. She rose from her chair, supple and silent as a cat. I had no idea why.

All the same, it seemed to me that the all-embracing look she gave him was definitely an answer.

I wanted to leave too. Standing in the middle of that circle of men and women, I felt ready to faint with embarrassment. Claudine noticed my misery and came back to my side; her sinewy hand gripped hold of mine and held it tight while my sister-in-law started asking me questions.

'Any news of Alain yet ?'

'No, not yet. Perhaps I'll find a telegram when I get home.'

'Well, good luck, and my blessing. Good-bye, Annie.'

'Where are you spending your holidays ?' Claudine asked me very gently.

'At Arriège, with Marthe and Léon.'

'As long as it's with Marthe ! . . . Alain can sail the seas without a qualm.'

'You don't imagine, that, even without Marthe . . .'

I realized I was blushing. Claudine shrugged her shoulders and replied, as she joined her husband who was waiting for her by the door with no sign of impatience :

'Good Lord, no ! He's trained you too well !'.

THREE

THAT telephone message of Marthe's embarrassed me considerably: 'Impossible to come and pick you up at home to go for a fitting at Taylor's. Come and fetch me at four o'clock at Claudine's.'

An indecent picture could not have upset me more than that piece of blue paper. At Claudine's! Marthe suggests it quite casually; the Timetable says ... What does it *not* say?

This appointment arranged by Marthe ... ought I to consider it as an official call on Renaud and Claudine? No ... Yes, of course ... I got in a state, and wondered whether to shuffle out of it, torn between the fear of offending my sister-in-law and the dread of Alain and my own conscience. However, my enfeebled conscience was too unsure of the right course to follow not to yield to the more immediate influence of Marthe. It yielded most of all to the delightful prospect of seeing this Claudine who is forbidden me like an outspoken, over-truthful book.

'Rue de Bassano, Charles.'

I had put on a dark, unassuming dress and I wore a plain net veil and neutral-tinted suède gloves, with the sole idea of removing any trace of 'official character' from my 'deportment'. I know how to use those words, for Alain's social experience has made me acutely conscious that, according to the occasion, one's 'deportment' should or should not assume an official character. When I mentally pronounce those words, they accompany a quaint, childish, puzzle-picture in the form of a caption ... Deportment, a little person with threadlike limbs, stretches out his arms towards the proffered sleeves of an

Academician's uniform, round whose collar 'official-characterofficialcharact ...' is embroidered in a delicate garland ... How silly I am to write all this down! It's only a little bit of maundering. I shall never put down my other maunderings; if I were to read them through again, this notebook would drop from my hands ...

On Claudine's landing, I glanced at my watch: ten past four. Marthe would be sure to have arrived and would be sitting nibbling sweets in that extraordinary drawing-room that I had hardly taken in on my earlier visits – I had been to suffocated by shyness.

'Is Madame Léon Payet here yet?'

A hostile old female servant gave me an absent-minded stare; she was far more interested in preventing a big brindled cat from escaping.

'Limaçon, just you wait ... I'll scorch your back-side for you, so I will ... Madame Léon ... what's her name? Floor below, very like.'

'No, I mean to say ... Is Madame Claudine at home?'

'So now it's Madame Claudine? You don't seem to know your own mind. Claudine, she lives here all right. But she's gone out.'

'Oh, you monstrous liar!' shouted a gay, tomboyish voice. 'I'm here and I'm at home. In one of your nasty moods, eh, Mélie?'

'No such thing,' retorted Mélie, unperturbed. 'But another time, you can open the door yourself. That'll larn you.'

And she retreated with much dignity, the tabby cat at her heels. I was left standing in the hall, waiting for some being to emerge from the shadows and be good enough to show me in ... Was this the witch's home? 'Sugar-house, sweet, pretty sugar-house ...' as Hansel and Gretel sang outside the alluring castle ...

'Come in! I'm in the drawing-room but I can't budge,' cried the same voice.

A tall shadow rose up and blotted out the window; it was Renaud coming to meet me.

'Come in, dear lady. The child's so desperately busy that she can't say how d'you do to you for a minute.'

The child? Ah, there she was, almost squatting on the hearth where a wood fire was blazing in spite of the season. I went forward, intrigued: she was holding out some mysterious object to the flames. More than ever, she made me think of the witch in the stories that frightened me and enraptured me in my credulous childhood. I half-feared, half-hoped to see strange creatures writhing in the flames that gilded Claudine's curly head – salamanders and tortured animals whose blood mingled with wine makes the victim languish to death...

She rose to her feet, perfectly calm.

'How d'you do, Annie.'

'How d'you do, Mad ... Claudine.'

It was a slight effort for me to address her by name. But it was impossible to say 'Madame' to this child-like young woman whom everyone called Claudine.

'It was just on the point of being done to a turn, so you see I couldn't possibly leave it.'

She was holding a little square grill made of silver wire on which a tablet of chocolate was blackening and swelling up. Toasted chocolate?

'You know, this utensil isn't perfect, even now, Renaud! They've made the handle too short and I've got a blister on my hand...'

'Show me quick.'

Her tall husband bent down, and tenderly kissed the slender, scorched hand, caressing it with his lips and fingers, like a lover ... They were no longer paying the slightest attention to me. I wondered whether I ought to go. This spectacle made me feel anything but inclined to laugh.

'All better!' cried Claudine, clapping her hands. 'We're going to eat our toasted chocolate now, Annie. Just the two of us. My great big beautiful man, I'm going to entertain a visitor in my drawing-room. Go into your study and see if I'm there.'

'Am I in the way, then?' that white-haired husband of hers whose eyes are those of a young man asked, still bending over her.

His wife stood on tiptoe, raised the ends of Renaud's long moustache with both hands and gave him a fierce, straining kiss. I was the one in the way. I got up to make my escape.

'Hi, Annie! Where are *you* rushing off to?'

A despotic hand grabbed hold of my arm and Claudine's ambiguous face with its mocking mouth and melancholy eyelids searched mine severely.

I blushed as if I felt guilty at having seen that kiss . . .

'I thought . . . I mean, since Marthe hasn't turned up . . .'

'Marthe? Is she supposed to be coming?'

'But of course! It was she who told me to come and meet her here . . . Otherwise . . .'

'What d'you mean – "otherwise" – you rude little thing? Renaud, did *you* know Marthe was supposed to be coming?'

'I did, darling.'

'You never mentioned it to *me*.'

'Sorry, little one. I read you all your letters in bed, as usual. But you were playing with Fanchette.'

'That's a barefaced lie. Why don't you admit *you* were tickling me all down my ribs with your nails? Sit *down*, Annie! Good-bye, you great bear . . .'

Renaud softly shut the door behind him.

I seated myself a little stiffly, right on the edge of the sofa. Claudine settled herself on it, tailor-fashion, with her legs drawn up and crossed under her orange cloth skirt. A supple white satin blouse, its whiteness emphasized by Japanese embroidery of the same colour as her skirt, gave a subtle glow to her matt complexion. What was she thinking of, all of a sudden so serious, sitting there pensively and looking like a little Bosphorus boatman with her embroidered skirt and her short hair?

'Beautiful, isn't he?'

I find her laconic utterances and her quick movements, as sudden and unexpected as her immobility, as shattering as blows.

'Who?'

'Renaud, of course. It's quite possible he did read me Marthe's letter . . . I couldn't have been paying attention.'

'He reads your letters?'

She gave a preoccupied nod; the tablet of toasted chocolate had stuck to the little silver grill and was threatening to crumble . . . Emboldened by her absent-mindedness, I asked:

'He reads them . . . before you do?'

The mischievous eyes looked up at me.

'Yes, Lovely-Eyes. (You don't mind my calling you "Lovely-Eyes"?) What's it got to do with you?'

'Nothing, of course. But I shouldn't like it myself.'

'On account of your beaux?'

'I don't have any beaux, Claudine!'

It burst from my lips with so much fervour, so much shocked sincerity that Claudine doubled herself up with delight.

'She's risen! She's risen! Oh, the simple soul! Well, Annie, I *have* had beaux . . . and Renaud used to read me their letters.'

'And . . . what did he say?'

'Oh . . . nothing. Not much, anyway. Occasionally he'd sigh: "Odd, Claudine, the number of people one meets who are convinced that they *aren't like everyone else* – and of the need to put it in writing." So that's that.'

'That's that . . .'

In spite of myself, I repeated the words in the same tone as hers.

'So it means nothing at all to you?'

'What? . . . Oh, all that . . . yes. In fact nothing means anything to me but one single human being . . .' She corrected herself . . . 'No, that's not true. I'm not indifferent to the sky being warm and clear. Or to cushions being deep enough to sink into and pamper my laziness, or to the year being rich in sweet apricots and floury chestnuts. I care passionately that the roof of my house in Montigny should be solid enough not to scatter its lichened tiles on a stormy day . . .' Her voice which had trailed away to a sing-song hastily recovered its firmness and went on ironically: 'As you see, Annie, I'm interested, like you and everyone else, in the external world. And, to speak as simply as your sophisticated novelist of a brother-in-law, "in what devouring time bears away on its changing restless tides".'

I shook my head, not quite sure that I believed her. Then, to please Claudine, I accepted scraps of grilled chocolate that tasted a little of smoke and very much of burnt sugar.

'Divine, isn't it? You know it was I who invented the chocolate grill, this nice little gadget that they've made, in spite of all my careful directions, with too short a handle. I also invented the flea-comb for Fanchette, the stove without holes for roasting winter chestnuts, pineapples in absinthe, and spinach tart . . . Mélie says *she*

did but it isn't true. I also invented my drawing-room –
kitchen which you see here.'

Claudine's humour made me alternate between
laughter and uneasiness. At one moment she troubled
me; the next I admired her. Her long tobacco-brown
eyes that ran right up to her temples had the same fervour, the same candid, direct look in them when she was
proclaiming her inventor's rights in the chocolate grill
as when she was proclaiming her passion for Renaud.

Her drawing-room kitchen added still further to this
disquieting impression. I wanted desperately to know
whether this woman I was talking to was an out-and-out
lunatic or an expert hoaxer.

It was like a kitchen or the public room of an inn, one
of those gloomy, smoky inns you find in Holland. But
where, on the wall of an inn, even a Dutch one, would
you find that exquisite, smiling fifteenth-century Virgin,
so enchanting in her pink tunic and blue mantle – a frail,
childish Madonna, on her knees yet seeming half-fright-
ened to pray ?

'It's beautiful, isn't it ?' said Claudine. 'But what I like
most about it is the vicious – yes, vicious is the only word
– contrast between that dress, all tender rosy pinks, and
that appalling, desolate landscape in the background. As
desolate as you were, Annie, the day your lord and
master Alain set sail. Don't you think about that voyager
any more now ?'

'Whatever do you mean ... not think about him any
more ?'

'Well, anyway, you don't think about him so much.
Oh, you needn't blush about it ... It's perfectly natural
when you've got an impeccable husband like yours ...
Just look at that Virgin's charmingly contrite expression;
she seems to be looking down at her baby Jesus and say-

27

ing, "Honestly, it's the very first time such a thing's happened to me!" Renaud thinks it's a Masolino. But the great Panjandrums of the art world attribute it to Filippo Lippi.'

'What do you think?'

'Me? I don't care a fig who painted it.'

I did not press the point. This very individual art critic rather disconcerted me.

In one corner, a Claudine in marble smiled under lowered eyelids like a St Sebastian who was revelling in his torments. A huge divan, covered with a dark bearskin that caressed my ungloved hand, retired into the shelter of a kind of alcove. But all the rest of the furniture astonished me; five or six public-house tables of shining dark oak and as many heavy, clumsy benches; an ancient rustic clock that did not go; some stone jugs, and a cavernous, canopied fireplace guarded by tall copper fire-dogs. Added to all this, the room was in a state of temporary disorder; books were strewn everywhere and gutted Reviews littered the dull rose carpet. Intrigued, I studied everything closely. It gave me a kind of melancholy ... the peculiar melancholy I associate with long voyages. I felt as if I had been staring for a long time through those small greenish panes, behind which the light was fading, at a grey ocean, flecked with a little foam, under a transparent veil of rain falling as lightly as fine ashes ...

Claudine had followed my thoughts and when I was back with her again we looked at each other with the same expression in our eyes.

'Do you like it here, Claudine?'

'Yes. I loathe bright, cheerful rooms. Here, I can travel. Look, those green walls are the glaucous colour of daylight seen through a wine-bottle. And those oak benches must have been polished by the depressed behinds of generations of poor wretches who only got drunk to drown their sorrows . . . I say, Annie, it looks as if Marthe isn't going to turn up. Typical of your precious sister-in-law, eh !'

How abruptly, almost brutally, she had snapped off the thread of her sad little reverie ! I had been following it so willingly, forgetting, just for this one hour, my anxiety about that husband of mine at sea . . . Besides, Claudine's changeableness was beginning to weary me with its mixture of childishness and savagery. I could not keep pace with the mind of this young barbarian that leapt in a flash from greed to shameless passion, from a despairing drunkard to that bustling, aggressive Marthe.

'Marthe . . . oh yes . . . She's very late.'

'I'll say she is ! No doubt Maugis has found some weighty reasons for keeping her.'

'Maugis ? Was she supposed to be seeing him today ?'

Claudine wrinkled up her nose, tilted her head sideways like an inquisitive bird, and stared deep into my eyes. Then she leapt to her feet and burst out laughing.

'I know nothing, I've seen nothing, I've heard nothing,' she cried like a voluble schoolgirl, jumping up and down. 'I'm only terrified of boring you. You've seen the chocolate grill, the drawing-room – kitchen, Renaud, the marble statue of me, the lot . . . Still I can call in Fanchette, can't I ?'

One never has time to answer Claudine. She opened a door, bent forward and chirruped mysterious summonses.

'My lovely, my precious, my snow-white . . . pussalina pussilove, mrrroo, mrrraow . . .'

The animal appeared, like a somnambulist, like a little wild beast under a spell. It was a very beautiful white she-cat who looked up at Claudine with green, obedient eyes.

'My little coalheaver, my little slut, you've gone and done weewee again on one of Renaud's patent-leather boots. Never mind, he won't know. I'll tell him its poor-quality leather. And he'll pretend to believe it. Come along and I'll read you some lovely things Lucie Delarue-Mardrus has written about cats.'

Claudine grabbed the cat by the scruff of the neck, lifted it high above her head and cried:

'Look, lady, the drowned cat hanging up on a hook!' She opened her fist and Fanchette fell from the height, landing expertly on her soft paws. Not in the least perturbed, she remained where she was on the carpet. 'You know, Annie, now that my girl lives in Paris, I read poetry to her. She knows everything Baudelaire has written about cats by heart. Now I'm teaching her all Lucie Delarue-Mardrus's cat poems.'

I smiled, amused at this inconsequent childishness.

'Do you think she understands?'

Claudine crushed me with a long, withering look over her shoulder.

'What an idiot you are, Annie! Sorry, I only meant to say: "Of course she does!" Sit Fanchette! Now just you watch and listen, you little sceptic. This one's unpublished ... It's marvellous ...:

'FOR A CAT

'Majestic cat, mysterious and wise,
Through whose black velvet mask gleam jewelled eyes,
Do my ring-laden fingers not presume too much,
When they caress you, monarch in disguise?

Lithe, furry serpent, coiled up in repose,
Warmer than living feathers to my touch
Save for the coolness where your small bare nose
Buds through the black and white, a glistening rose.

Jungle-fierce still for all your ribbon bows
And feigned docility. Let some hapless toy

Catch your disdainful eye, at once peremptory paws
Pounce on the prey grappling-irons of claws.

Tonight, here in the dusk, no wile of mine
Can lure your still remoteness, make you
  glance from where
You sit, a Buddha-cat of stone, gold eyes astare:
You are remembering you were once divine.'

The cat was half-asleep, vibrating with a faint, muffled
purr that made a muted accompaniment to Claudine's
peculiar voice, now grave and full of harshly rolled *r*'s,
now so soft and low that it sent a shiver down my spine
. . . When the voice ceased, Fanchette opened her slant-
ing eyes. The two gazed at each other for a moment with
the same grave intentness . . . Then raising her forefinger
and touching her nose, Claudine turned to me and
sighed:

'"Peremptory . . ." It took some finding, that word!
They're good, aren't they, those verses of Fervid's. Just
to have hit on "peremptory", *I'd* gladly give ten years
. . . of the Chessenet's life!'

That name seemed as shockingly inappropriate here
as a piece of gimcrack in a flawless collection.

'You don't like Ch . . . Madame Chessenet, Claudine?'

Claudine, now semi-recumbent, stared at the ceiling
and put up a lazy hand.

'She means nothing to me . . . A carved yellow beetroot
. . . Means no more to me than the Cabbage-Rose.'

'Ah, the Cabbage-Rose . . .'

'Rose or cabbage? That buxom girl with cheeks like
the buttocks of little Cupids.'

'Oh!'

'Why that shocked "Oh!"? Buttocks isn't a dirty
word. Anyway the Cabbage-Rose bores me too . . .' She
yawned.

31

'And . . . Marthe ?'

I was animated by an indiscreet curiosity, as if, by questioning Claudine, I was about to discover the secret, the 'recipe' of her lucky disposition that detached her from everything, and made her indifferent to gossip, petty quarrels, even to the conventions. But I was not adroit enough and Claudine made fun of me. With a carp-like leap, she turned over on her stomach and said mockingly, with her nose in her cat's silvery fur:

'Marthe ? I think she's missed her appointment . . . I mean the one she made with us. But . . . is this an interrogation, Annie ?'

I was ashamed. I leant towards her and said, in a sudden burst of frankness:

'Forgive me, Claudine. The fact is I was beating about the bush . . . I couldn't bring myself to ask you . . . what you think of Alain . . . Ever since he went away, I just haven't known how to go on living and nobody talks to me about him, at least not in the way I want them to talk . . . Is it usual in Paris to forget people so quickly when they've gone away ?'

I had come straight out with what was in my mind, and I was surprised at my own vehemence. Claudine's triangular face, propped up on two small fists, its smooth rather sallow skin lightened by pearly reflections from the white satin blouse, took on a wary expression.

'Is it usual to forget ? . . . I don't really know. I suppose it depends on the person who goes away. As a husband, Monsieur Samzun – "Alain" as you call him – impresses me as . . . impeccable. As a man ? He aims at being distinguished, but all he manages to be is correct. He's always talking in aphorisms . . . no man ever had such a store of them. And his whole manner, all his typical gestures are highly . . .'

'"Peremptory",' I said with a timid smile.

'Yes, but *he* hasn't any right to be "peremptory" because he isn't a cat. No, he most certainly isn't a cat! He's got snobbery in his heart and a ramrod in his arse ... Heavens, what an idiot I am! For goodness' sake, don't start crying as if I'd hit you, my poor child! As if it mattered what *I* say! You know perfectly well, that Claudine's got a hole in her head ... Oh, very well then, she wants to go! Kiss me first to show me there's no ill-feeling. Do you know what she looks like with her great knot of hair and her straight little frock and those dew-drops on the end of her lashes? A little girl who's been married against her will!'

I smiled to please her, to thank her too for giving me a glimpse of her honest, rebellious mind instead of the conventional lies I was used to.

'Good-bye, Claudine ... I'm not angry with you.'

'I should hope not. Will you give me a kiss?'

'Oh yes!'

Her tall flexible body bent over me; she laid both hands on my shoulders.

'Put up your mouth! Goodness, what am I saying ...? Force of habit ... Put up your cheek. There! See you soon, in Arriège? This is the way out. Remember me to that trollop of a Marthe. No, your eyes aren't red. Good-bye, good-bye ... chrysalis!'

I went down the stairs slowly, pausing on every step, irresolute and disturbed. She had said: 'A ramrod in his ...' Honestly, I believe it was the metaphor, the picture of that ramrod that had shocked me, not Claudine's opinion in itself. She had blasphemed and, abashed for a moment in the presence of this uninhibited child, I had let her blaspheme.

My dear Alain,
 I promised you to show I could be brave. So I'll only

show you my brave side . . . forgive me for hiding all the other. You can guess it only too well.

I've done everything I possibly can to see that our home that you like to be tidy and properly kept up isn't suffering too much from your absence. I go through the servants' books on the appointed day and Léonie is being very kind to me . . . that is to say, I am sure her intentions are good, anyway.

Your sister is charming, as usual. Seeing her as much as I do, I wish I could acquire a little of her courage and her never-failing will-power. However, I won't pretend that this isn't a very lofty ambition. Anyway, you don't really want me to be like that and you are so intelligent and strong-minded yourself that it's more than enough for the two of us.

I don't know where this letter will reach you and this feeling of uncertainty makes me all the more nervous and awkward when I write to you. A correspondence between us is something so new to me now; I've got so much out of the habit of it. I wish I need never have to get into the habit again. Yet I realize that, in my weak moments, it will be my one great stay and comfort. I can only say in a few words, putting it badly, I am sure, and saying much less than I think, that my heart follows you wherever you go with all my devoted love, and that I remain

Your little slave,

Annie

I wrote this letter with extreme constraint, without ever letting my love and grief burst out spontaneously to him. Was it lack of confidence in myself, as usual, or, for the first time, in *him*?

Which Annie would he prefer? The Annie, softer and more silent than a feather; the one he knew, the one he had accustomed to be mute, to veil her thoughts under

34

her words as she veiled her eyes under lashes or the lost, troubled Annie, defenceless against her crazy imagination, whom he has left behind here – the Annie he does not know?

Whom he does not know . . .

Letting my thoughts run on like this, I feel guilty. Hiding something is almost like lying. I have no right to hide two Annies in myself. Suppose the second were only half of the other? How exhausting this all is!

As for Alain, you know the whole of him when you've known him an hour. His mind is as regular as his face. He detests the illogical and dreads the unconventional. Would he have married me, if one evening long ago when we were engaged I had flung my arms round his neck and said: 'Alain, I can't endure another minute unless you make love to me . . .'?

The mere fact of his being away is upsetting my reason. Already there are so many tormenting thoughts that I must not admit to him when he returns. This is not going to be anything like the 'Diary of his journey' I was expected to keep: it will be the diary of a wretched, distraught creature . . .

'Madame, a telegram!'

That brusque military manner of Léonie's frightened me. My fingers are still trembling with apprehension.

Excellent journey. Sailing today. Letter follows. Affectionate thoughts.

                                        Samzun

Was that all? A telegram is not a letter and this one should have reassured me on every vital point. But it arrived at a moment when I was completely demoralized. Somehow, I would have liked something very different. Besides, I don't like his signing himself 'Samzun'. Do I sign myself 'Lajarrisse'? My poor Annie, what hornet

35

has stung you today ? And what madness to go and compare yourself to a man . . . to a man like Alain !

I shall go and see Marthe to escape from myself.

When I arrived, it was Léon I found at home. As every day, at this time, he was busy in his study which Marthe calls 'the torture-chamber'. Bookcases with gilded latticework, a beautiful Louis XVI table on which this model writer never lets a drop of ink spill, for he writes carefully, with a blotter under his hand . . . altogether a very commodious prison.

As I entered, he rose and dabbed his temples.

'This heat, Annie ! I can't produce anything the least good in it. Besides, somehow, it's a languid, depressing day in spite of the sunshine. A bad, immoral day.'

'It is, isn't it ?' I broke in eagerly, almost gratefully. He stared at me with his beautiful spaniel-like eyes, without the faintest idea what I meant . . .

'Yes, I'm going to find it hard to grind out my sixty lines today.'

'You'll be scolded, Léon.'

He languidly shrugged his shoulders, as if inured to it.

'How's your novel going ? Well ?'

Pulling his pointed beard, he answered with a vanity as discreet as his modest talent :

'Not too badly . . . much as the others.'

'Tell me how it's going to end.'

Léon appreciates me as a willing, easily-interested audience. I have at least managed to acquire a taste, however mild, for his tales of adulteresses in high society and noble suicides and princely bankrupts . . .

'The end's giving me a good deal of trouble,' sighed my unhappy brother-in-law. 'The husband has taken his wife back, but she's tasted freedom and found it intoxicating. It would be better, from the literary point of

36

view, if she stayed with him. But, as Marthe points out, it would sell better if she went off again and hopped into bed with someone else.'

Léon has retained some expressions from his journalist days that I find quite revolting.

I said: 'The point is, does she want to go off?'

'Of course she does!'

'Well, then, she must.'

'Why?'

'Because she's "tasted freedom".'

Léon sniggered as he continued to count his pages.

'That sounds funny ... coming from you, of all people! ... Marthe's waiting for you at the Fritz,' he went on, picking up his pen again. 'Forgive me for hustling you off, Annie dear, won't you? I've got to deliver this thing in October, so ...'

He indicated the still meagre pile of manuscript.

'Yes, of course ... Get on with your work, poor old Léon.'

'Place Vendôme, Charles!'

Marthe has become passionately addicted to these five o'clock teas in the Fritz. I infinitely prefer my little 'Afternoon Tea' in the Rue d'Indy with its low-ceilinged room that smells of cake and ginger, and its mixed clientele of elderly English ladies in sham pearl necklaces, and demi-mondaines who use it for discreet assignations.

Marthe, however, loves that long white gallery at the Fritz. She walks through it, peering about as if she were short-sighted and were searching for someone when, all the time, from the moment she entered, her menacing grey eyes have been taking in every detail. She has been counting the people there and summing them up; noting familiar faces and scanning them sharply; noting, most

37

of all, the hats she will copy with that infallible hand when she gets home.

What a horrible nature I have! Here I am, thinking almost spitefully of my sister-in-law whose company has cheered me up and distracted me ever since Alain went away ... The fact is, I tremble every time I have to walk by myself down that redoubtable gallery at the Fritz, under the eyes of those people devouring little cakes and even more eagerly devouring their neighbours.

Once again, I launched myself into that rectangular hall with the foolhardiness of the very shy and traversed it with long strides, thinking with terror: 'I'm going to catch my foot in my dress and twist my ankle ... perhaps my placket-hole is gaping, I'm sure my hair is coming down at the back ...' I was so preoccupied that I walked right past Marthe without seeing her.

She caught me by the crook of her parasol and laughed so uproariously that I thought I would die of shame.

'Who are you running after, Annie? You look like a woman hurrying guiltily to her first assignation. There, there, sit down, give me your parasol, take off your gloves ... Ouf! Saved once again in the nick of time! I must say that little face could be a lot worse, even if you *are* in torture. It suits you to look scared to death. Who were you running away from?'

'Everybody.'

She contemplated me with pitying disdain and sighed:

'I've almost given up hope of ever making anything of you. Do you like my hat?'

'Yes.'

I said it with genuine conviction.

Till then, I had been too busy pulling myself together to look at Marthe. I suppose you could, by stretching a point, call it a hat, that muslin mob-cap, falling in pleats round the face? Hat or not, it 'came off'. The linen dress, the inevitable fichu that revealed the milky neck, completed a charming fancy-dress of the French Revolution period. She was still Marie-Antoinette, but already in the Temple prison. Never would I have dared to go out arrayed like that!

Radiating with self-confidence, she flashed her formidable eyes all about her; there were not many men who could sustain those glances. As she crunched her toast with relish, she stared at people, chattered and simultaneously reassured me and dazed me.

'Did you look in at our place?'

'Yes . . .'

'Did you see Léon?'

'Yes.'

'Was he working?'

'Yes.'

'He mustn't let up, the thing's simply got to be in in October. I've got some heavy bills . . . Any news of Alain?'

'A telegram . . . he says there's a letter coming.'

'You know we're leaving in five days time?'

'Whenever you like, Marthe.'

'"Whenever you like"! Honestly, you wear me out, my good girl! Look, quick, there's the Cabbage-Rose. Her hat's a disaster!'

Hats play a considerable part in my sister-in-law's life. Moreover, it was undeniable that the hat the Cabbage-Rose (a lovely, fresh, slightly overblown creature) was wearing *was* an utter failure.

Marthe wriggled with delight.

'And she wants us to believe that she ruins herself buying her hats at Reboux! The Chessenet, who's her best friend, told me the Cabbage-Rose cuts all the labels out of her mother-in-law's smart hats and sews them inside her own.'

'Do you believe that?'

'One should always believe the worst first go, there's always time to find out the facts later ... What luck! Here come the Renaud – Claudines ... we'll call them over to our table. Maugis is with them.'

'But, Marthe ...'

'But what?'

'Alain doesn't like us to see too much of the Renaud – Claudines.'

'I'm quite aware of that.'

'So I oughtn't to ...'

'Since your husband isn't here, stop worrying ... I'm the one who invited you, so you're relieved of all responsibility ...'

After all, since Marthe *was* my hostess ... my Timetable might forgive me!

Claudine had seen us. From a yard away, she greeted Marthe with a resounding: 'All hail, Goldilocks!' that made heads turn in our direction.

Renaud followed her, indulgent as usual to all her crazy ways, and Maugis brought up the rear. I don't much like that Maugis, but I put up with his cheerful drunken effrontery and now and then find it amusing. I shan't say a word to Alain about this meeting; being so sober and correct himself, he positively abhors this great fat untidy Bohemian who always wears a stove-pipe top-hat.

Marthe fluttered like a white hen.

'Claudine, will you have tea?'

'Ugh, not tea! It turns my stomach.'

'Chocolate?'

'No. I'd like some cheap wine. The twelve sous a litre kind.'

'Some *what*?' I asked, staggered.

'Ssh, Claudine!' Renaud gently remonstrated, smiling

under his whitening moustache. 'You'll scandalize Madame Samzun.'

'Why?' exclaimed Claudine. 'What's wrong with wine at twelve sous a . . .'

'Not here, my pet. You and I will go off and have some on our own. We'll drink it, with our elbows propped on the zinc counter of that little pub in the Avenue Trudaine – the one with the shady but extremely affable proprietor. Would you like that – ' (he dropped his voice) '– my darling bird?'

'Oh yes, yes! Oh, I'd adore it!' cried the incorrigible Claudine.

She gazed at her husband with so much childish enthusiasm and loving admiration that I was suddenly choked with an overwhelming desire to cry. If I had asked Alain for wine that cost twelve sous a litre he would have given me . . . permission to go to bed and take some bromide!

Maugis dropped his moustache towards me, a moustache bleached by a cosmopolitan taste in liquor.

'Madame, you appear to be suffering certain pangs of remorse occasioned by this tepid tea and these vomitively chocolatious éclairs . . . You most certainly will not be able to imbibe the necessary cordial here at the Fritz. The liquid refreshments they serve here would wreck the livers of hardened drinkers in the lowest type of military canteen . . . I cannot say the sixty-centime claret recommended by Madame Claudine excites me either, except to cynical merriment . . . What *you* need is a nice green.'

'A nice what?'

'Call it blue, if that appeals to you more. A Pernod for babies. I am the president of a Feminist Society: "The Right to Absinthe". I can tell you the members don't half put it away.'

'I've never drunk absinthe in my life,' I said with some disgust.

'Oh!' exclaimed Claudine, 'there are so many things you've never tasted, good little Annie!'

She put so much meaning into the words that she made me feel foolish and embarrassed. With a laugh, she gave a mocking glance at Marthe who replied:

'She needs educating. We're counting a lot on "the easy relaxed life of fashionable watering-places", as someone puts it in Léon's latest novel.'

'In *The Tragic Hearts*?' exclaimed Maugis effusively. 'A powerful work, Madame, and one that will live. The torments of an ill-starred but aristocratic love affair are depicted in letters of fire by a pen dipped in gall!'

To my amazement, Marthe burst out laughing. There they were, all four of them, making fun of that poor, wretched man back at home, grinding out his daily sixty lines. I was embarrassed and shocked, yet forced to seem amused in self-defence. I studied the bottom of my cup, then I furtively glanced up at Claudine who happened to be looking at me and who murmured very low to her husband, as if she were talking to herself:

'What marvellous eyes Annie's got, hasn't she, Renaud dear? Wild chicory flowers, growing out of brown sand . . . .'

'Yes,' agreed Renaud, and added: 'When she raises her eyelids it's as if she were taking off her clothes.'

All four stared at me with a far-away expression. I suffered agonies of shame, coupled with agonies of appalling pleasure, as if my dress had suddenly dropped off.

Marthe was the first to pull herself together and change the conversation.

'When will you two be coming down there?' she asked Renaud and Claudine.

'Down where, my dear Marthe?'

'To Arriège, naturally. It's a sad fact, but nowadays all good Parisians harbour a sleeping arthritic under their skin.'

'Mine suffers from insomnia,' said Maugis pompously. 'I douse it with whisky. But you and your cures, that's all a lot of chichi, lady Marthe. You just want to be in the fashion.'

'Not at all, you insolent man! I take Arriège very seriously. Those four weeks of treatment set me up for the winter so that I can eat truffles, drink Burgundy, and go to bed at three in the morning ... Talking of that, it is next Tuesday, isn't it, that we all make our pilgrimage to the shrine of the Lalcade? It should be a good party, much gayer than Arriège.'

'Oh, certainly,' replied Claudine. 'It'll be crammed with dukes, with some princes thrown in for good measure. You'd go if you had to stand on your head, wouldn't you, Marthe?'

'I could stand on my head here and now,' said Marthe rather superciliously. 'My underclothes are nice enough to survive it ...'

'And besides,' Maugis grumbled into his moustache, 'she wears closed knickers.'

I had heard. We had all heard!

There was a brief, chilly silence.

'What about you, pensive one?' Claudine was asking. 'Are you Arrièging?'

The 'pensive one' was myself ... I started ... I was already far away.

'Me? Oh, I shall follow Marthe and Léon.'

'And I shall follow Renaud to see he doesn't follow other petticoats (I'm only joking, dearest!). What luck! We'll meet again down there. I shall watch you all drinking water that tastes of rotten eggs and be able to compare your respective grimaces and know which of you has the most stoical soul. *Your* face should be a study taking the waters, Maugis, you bloated old wineskin.'

They laughed, but I had an anguished vision of how Alain's face would look if he suddenly came in and saw me in such improper company. For after all, Marthe's presence doesn't justify everything and one really can't be on intimate terms with that crazy Claudine who calls people 'bloated old wine-skins'.

'Alain, I shan't go to Madame Lalcade's.'

'You must go, Annie.'

'But I shall be so lonely, so sad with you not there.'

'So sad . . . my modesty prefers not to discuss that. But not lonely. Marthe and Léon will escort you.'

'I'll go if you want me to.'

'Do try and develop a little social sense, dear child, and not regard every function I consider it expedient for you to attend as some kind of dreary duty. This party of Madame Lalcade's will be reckoned as a . . . a manifesto of art and your absence will delight certain ill-natured people . . . Don't neglect this very agreeable house, perhaps the only one where people in society can safely rub elbows with any number of interesting artists . . . If you knew how to put yourself forward a little more, you might get yourself introduced to the Comtesse Greffulhe . . .'

'Ah?'

'But I haven't much hope, that, especially without me, you'll be able to do yourself justice . . . Ah well!'

'What ought I to wear?'

'Your white dress with the shirring at the waist seems to me to be indicated. Great simplicity, that night, Annie.

44

You'll see a slight excess of Gismonda coiffures and Laparcerie dresses at Madame Lalcade's ... There must be absolutely nothing about your appearance to warrant your feeling embarrassed ... Be just as you are now, simple, reserved, unaffected; don't add anything, don't change anything. Isn't that a handsome compliment I'm paying you?'

A very handsome one, certainly, and I fully appreciated its worth.

That conversation took place a fortnight ago and I can still hear every word Alain said in that firm, unhesitating voice of his.

Tonight I shall put on my white dress and I shall go to Madame Lalcade's party and listen to Fauré's sad and frivolous music which is to be mimed by people in fancy-dress ... I am thinking of Marthe's delight. She is replacing, almost at the last moment, a pretty Marquise who has a cold. In forty-eight hours, my sister-in-law has confected something out of shimmering silks, tried on a whalebone bodice, consulted engravings and hairdressers, and rehearsed a rigadoon.

'What a crowd of people, Léon!'

'Yes. I recognized the Voronsoffs' carriage and the Gourkaus' and the ... Be so kind as to button my glove, Annie ...'

'Your gloves are terribly tight!'

'Not tight, Annie, only new. The woman at the glove-shop always says to me "Monsieur's hands seem to get smaller and smaller" ...'

I did not even smile at his childishness. Vain of his hands and feet, my poor brother-in-law endures a thousand small tortures but will not concede even a quarter of a size to his mangled fingers.

Such a flood of light wraps overflowed through the

door of the conservatory being used as a cloakroom and right out into the garden, that, for a minute, I was agitated by the fear and the hope that I would not be able to get into it ... Léon forced a slow passage for me through the crowd with an insinuating elbow. Obviously I should get in but my dress would be ruined ... I looked frantically for a corner of a looking-glass, quite convinced that my heavy knot of hair was coming undone ... Between two sumptuous dowdies, I caught a glimpse of a fragment of myself. Yes, that was Annie, slim and brown as a coloured girl ... those were her blue eyes, blue as the turned-down gas-flame, so meekly submissive they seemed to be treacherous.

'All's well, all's well. Very much in form, tonight, the whipped child!'

Now the mirror reflected, quite close to mine, Claudine's vigorous profile and the sharp-pointed *décolletage* of her yellow dress that rippled like a flame ...

I turned round to ask her, idiotically enough: 'I've lost Léon ... You haven't seen him?'

The yellow female fiend burst out laughing.

'Truth and honour, I haven't got him on me! Are you really in such a desperate state?'

'About what?'

'About mislaying your brother-in-law.'

'It's just ... You see, Marthe's playing in this mime and I haven't anyone but him.'

'Perhaps he's dead,' said Claudine with macabre solemnity. 'It's of no importance. I'll chaperon you just as well. We'll sit down, we'll look at the greasy shoulders of old ladies, we'll hit them over the head if they talk during the music, and I shall eat all the strawberries on the buffet!'

This alluring programme (or was it Claudine's irresistible authority?) decided me. With my head bent low,

I made my first step into the studio where Madame Lalcade paints and gives parties. It was filled to overflowing with massed flowers and human beings.

'She's invited all her models,' whispered my companion.

It was glittering with women, so closely packed that, at each sensational new arrival, only their heads turned and nodded like a field of heavy poppies in the wind.

'Claudine, we'll never be able to sit down in there ...'

'Oh yes we shall. Just you wait!'

Claudine's smiling unceremoniousness admitted no rebuff. She conquered half a chair, agitated her hips till she had invaded the whole of it, and installed me, heaven knows how, beside her.

'There! Look-see the pretty stage-curtain with the garlands. Oh, how I love everything you can't see behind! Look-see also Valentine Chessenet in red with her rabbit's eyes also in red ... Honestly, has Marthe got a part? Look-see again, Annie, there's Madame Lalcade saying how d'you do to us over fifty-three ladies. How d'you do, too, Madame? How d'you do, Madame! Yes, yes, we're very well, thank you. Three quarters of our behinds have somewhere to lay their head.'

'People will hear you, Claudine!'

'Let them hear me!' retorted the redoubtable creature. 'I'm not saying anything dirty. My heart is pure and I wash every day. So there! How d'you do, Maugis, you great tun-belly! He's come to see Marthe *décolletée* to her very soul and possibly for the music as well ... Oh, how lovely the Cabbage-Rose is tonight! I defy you, Annie, to distinguish from a yard away where her skin ends and her pink dress begins. And what healthy, abundant meat. At four sous a pound there must be a hundred thousand francs' worth! No, don't try and work out how many kilos that makes ... Look, there's Renaud over there in that doorway.'

Without her realizing it, her voice had all at once softened.

'I can't see anything.'

'Neither can I, except the tip of a moustache, but I know it's his.'

Yes, she knew it was he. Passionate, instinctive animal that she is, she could pick up his scent, through all those other warm effluences, all those perfumes, all those breaths ... Why is it that every time I am forcibly reminded of their love, I feel unbearably sad ?

The electric lights suddenly went out. There was that *Ah!* of vulgar surprise that bursts from the crowd when the first firework goes off on the fourteenth of July, followed by enraged chattering. Then that too was abruptly quenched ... On the still invisible stage, harps were already pattering like raindrops; plucked mandolines were softly twanging an invocation: 'Come, all you fair ladies ...' Then, slowly, the curtain rose.

'Oh, this is bliss,' Claudine whispered, enraptured. Against a grey-tinted backcloth of a formal park, Aminte, Tircis, and Clitandre, the Abbé, the Ingénue, and the Roué, lay about in languorous attitudes as if just returned from Cythera. The swing hardly swayed under the light weight of a panniered shepherdess at whom a shepherd in reddish-purple gazed up adoringly. An exquisite creature turned over the pages of a music-book, bent forward so low that her charms were exposed as she followed the song her lover's languid fingers were tracing ... Far too soon, all this enchantment – the disillusioned dreamers, the sweetly ironical music – was dispersed by the lively chords that announced the rigadoon.

'What a pity !' sighed Claudine.

Grave couples in shimmering costumes paraded, pirouetted, curtsied and bowed. The last Marquise, all in frosty silver on the arm of a sky-blue Marquis, was Marthe, so dazzling that a murmur greeted her appearance and I could hardly believe it was she.

The will to be beautiful had transfigured her. Here and there the fire of her hair glinted through the ash of powder that could not extinguish it. With her eyes burning paler against her make-up, her firm round breasts disclosed almost beyond the limits of decency, her face serious and concentrated, she pivoted on perilous pointed heels, plunged into curtsies, raised her little painted hand and, at each pirouette, darted her most terrible Ninon-turned-anarchist glance at the audience ... With no real beauty and no more than superficial grace, Marthe eclipsed all the pretty women who danced alongside her.

She *willed* to be the most beautiful ... Such a thing would be impossible to a poor creature like me. The sad, pompous music mocked me, melted me, moved me to the point of tears. But my self-consciousness would not let me indulge my feelings. Everything was ruined for me by the effort to stop myself crying, by the thought of the cruel lights that would go on in a moment and of Claudine's too-penetrating gaze.

My very dear Annie,

Your letter arrived just before I sailed so if this one is brief, you must blame it entirely on the hurry of departure. I am delighted to know you are showing yourself to be so courageous and so attached to everything that makes up the life of a simple woman in good society: your husband, your family, your charming well-kept and well-ordered home.

For it seems to me that, being away from you, I may,

perhaps even should, pay you the compliments I refrain from paying you when I am with you. Do not thank me for it, Annie, for, to some extent, it is my own work I am admiring; a lovable child, fashioned little by little and without great difficulty into an irreproachable young woman and an accomplished housewife.

The weather is superb; we can count on a perfect crossing. So you can hope that everything will proceed normally till I reach Buenos Aires. You know that my health is excellent and that the sun has no terrors for me. Therefore you must not fret if the posts are rare and irregular. I shall contain myself and not await your letters too impatiently, though they will nevertheless be precious when they arrive.

I embrace you, my very dear Annie, with all my un-shakeable affection. I know you will not smile at my rather solemn form of expression; the feeling that attaches me to you has nothing frivolous about it.

Your
Alain Samzun

With my forefinger pressed to one throbbing temple, it was a labour to read his letter. For once again I was in the grip of that prostrating migraine that recurs at almost regular intervals to make life a misery. With my jaws clenched and my left eye closed, I listened to an incessant hammer in my wretched brain. Daylight hurts me: darkness stifles me.

In the old days, at my grandmother's, I used to inhale ether till I almost lost consciousness. But, during the first months of our marriage, Alain found me one day half-swooning on my bed, with a bottle clutched in my hand, and he forbade me ever to use it again. He spoke to me very seriously and lucidly about the dangers of ether, about his horror of these 'hysterics' remedies', about the harmlessness, in short, of migraines: 'All women have them!' Ever since, I have endured the pain with as much patience as I could muster, limiting myself, quite unsuccessfully, to hot compresses and general hydrotherapy.

But today I was suffering so much that I wanted to cry. The sight of certain white objects, a piece of paper, an enamelled table, the sheets of the bed on which I was lying produced that contraction of the throat and that nervous nausea I know and dread only too well. Alain's letter . . . so longed for, none the less! . . . seemed to me cold and colourless. I realized this must be a really vicious attack . . . I would re-read the letter later.

Léonie came in. She took great care not to make a noise: she opened the door very softly, but banged it loudly behind her. At least her intentions were good.

'Is Madame's head still bad?'

'Yes, Léonie . . .'

'Why doesn't Madame take . . . ?'

'A glass of brandy? No, thank you.'

'No, Madame, a little ether.'

'Monsieur doesn't like me to drug myself, Léonie. Ether won't help me.'

'It's Monsieur who makes Madame believe that. Monsieur is a nice man in every way and he imagines it might do Madame harm, but, when it comes to knowing anything about women's troubles, don't you talk to me of men. *I* always take ether when I get my neuralgia.'

'Ah! You . . . you've actually got some here?'

'A brand-new bottle. I'll go and fetch it for Madame.'

The divine, powerful odour relaxed my nerves. I lay back full-length on my bed, the bottle under my nostrils, weeping tears of weakness and pleasure. The cruel blacksmith retreated, there was only a discreet padded finger tapping my temple now. I breathed in so hard that there was a sweet taste in my throat . . . my wrists turned heavy.

There followed vague, fleeting dreams, all barred by a line of light – the one that filtered through my half-closed eyelids. I saw Alain in a tennis shirt he wore one summer eight years ago, a white cellular one that his flesh tinted pink ... I myself was the very young Annie of those days, with my heavy plait that ended in a soft ringlet ... I touched the supple flesh of the pink shirt and it excited me like living skin, warm as my own, and I told myself confusedly that Alain was a little boy and it didn't matter, didn't matter, didn't matter ... He was passive and vibrant; over his burning cheeks he drooped long black lashes that were Annie's eyelashes ... How velvety that skin felt to the touch! Didn't matter ... didn't matter ...

But a tennis-ball suddenly hit me hard on the temple and I caught it in flight. It was warm and white ... a nasal voice, quite close to me, announced: 'It's a cock's egg.' I was not in the least surprised, since Alain was now a cock, a red cock on the bottom of a plate. He scratched the china with an arrogant claw till it squeaked maddeningly and crowed '*I* always ...' What was he saying? I couldn't hear. The bar of greyish-blue light cut him in half like the President of the Republic's sash. Then came blackness, blackness, a delicious death, a slow falling sustained by wings ...

A wicked act, a wicked act, yes Annie, there is no other word for it! A piece of deliberate, complete disobedience to Alain's will. He was right to forbid me this ether that makes me quite irresponsible ... Thus I accused myself in all humility two hours later, alone with my own reflection in the glass, sitting at my dressing-table where I was brushing and re-doing my dishevelled hair. My head was free, clear and empty. Only the dark circles under my eyes, my pale lips, and my lack of appetite, though I had been fasting all day, gave evidence of my debauch with the beloved poison. Ugh! The stale, cold fumes of ether clung to the curtains. I must have air, I must forget – if I could . . .

My window, on the second floor, has a dismal outlook. I opened it and gazed at the narrow courtyard where Alain's horse was being rubbed down by a stout groom in a check shirt. At the sound of my window being opened, a black bull terrier sitting on the cobbles raised his square muzzle . . . It was my poor Toby, my banished, disgraced Toby! The next second, he was on his feet, a small dark figure, waving the remnant of his cropped tail at me.

'Toby! Toby!'

He jumped up and down, making wheezy little grunts like moans. I leant out.

'Charles, send Toby up to me by the back stairs, please.'

Toby had understood before the man and bounded forward. Another minute and the poor black French bull-dog was at my feet, in a delirious convulsion of humility and love, his eyes and his tongue nearly bursting out of his head.

I had bought him last year from one of Jacques Delavalise's stablemen, because he was really a beautiful little eight-month-old bull-pup with an uncropped tail, no nose, limpid slits of eyes and ears like trumpets. And I had brought him home, feeling rather proud but slightly apprehensive. Alain examined him with an expert but not unfriendly eye.

'A hundred francs, you say? That's not dear. The coachman will be pleased, the rats are destroying everything in the stable.'

'In the stable! But that's not what I bought him for. He's pretty. I wanted to keep him for myself, Alain.'

'For yourself? A stable bulldog in a Louis XV drawing-room ? Or on the lace covers of your bed ? If you really want a dog, my dear child, I'll find you a little floss-silk Havanese for the drawing-room, or perhaps a big Saluki . . . Salukis go with all styles.'

He rang the bell and, when Jules appeared, he indicated my poor black Toby who was innocently chewing the knob of a chair.

'Take this dog to Charles, say he's to buy him a collar, keep him clean and tell me if he's a good ratter. The dog is called Toby.'

Since then I have never seen Toby, except through the window. I had watched him suffering and thinking of me, for we had loved each other at sight.

One day, I kept back some little pigeon bones and carried them out to him in the yard, taking care no one saw him. I came back indoors with a heavy heart and with an uneasy feeling I thought I could dissipate by confessing my weakness to Alain. He hardly scolded me at all.

'What a child you are, Annie! If you like, I'll tell Charles he can take the bull-terrier with him under the seat sometimes when you go out in the carriage. But don't let me ever find Toby in the flat, will you ? Never, is that understood ? You'll oblige me greatly by remembering this.'

Today, admitting to Alain that I had let Toby into my bedroom would not be enough to relieve me of all anxiety – I may as well be frank – of all remorse. This crime which, last week, would have made me tremble, is a trifle compared to my guilty, delicious ether-intoxication.

Go on sleeping on the carpet patterned with grey roses, black Toby; go on sleeping with the great sighs of an animal worn out by emotion : you are not going back to the stable.

FOUR

Arriège.

A smell of orange-blossom and sulphur baths comes up through my open window. 'The local smell,' the hotel porter who brought up our luggage obligingly explained to me. Marthe assures me one gets used to it in a couple of days. To the scent of the flowering oranges planted in a hedge in front of the hotel, granted. But the other, that sulphurous smell that clings to one's very skin, it's revolting!

I leant on the sill, already discouraged, while Léonie whose felt travelling hat made her look like a policeman in mufti unpacked my great wicker trunk and disposed the silver trinkets from my dressing-case like soldiers on parade.

What on earth was I doing here? I felt less alone in Paris, in my yellow bedroom with Alain's portrait for company, than between these four walls distempered in pink with an undertone of grey. A brass bed whose weary mattress and bedclothes I have inspected suspiciously. A dressing-table that is too small, a writing-desk I shall use to do my hair at, a folding-table I shall use to write on, some commonplace upholstered chairs and some white-painted wooden ones. How many days had I got to live in this room? Marthe had said: 'That all depends.'

From the other side of the flagged corridor, I heard her piercing voice. Léon's muffled replies, which I could not catch, made a blank between her remarks. I sank into a torpor, isolated from everything, from the place I was in, from Marthe, from Alain, from the disturbing future, from all sense of passing time . . .

'Shall we go down, Annie?'

'Oh, Marthe! You gave me a fright! But I'm not ready!'

'Good heavens, whatever do you imagine you're doing? Not even got washed or done your hair? For mercy's sake, don't start being a dead weight the moment you get here.'

My sister-in-law was arrayed as if for the Fritz, fresh, made-up and rosy. Eleven hours of railway journey had dealt kindly with her. She declared she wanted to go and listen to the music in the park.

'I'll hurry up. What about Léon?'

'He's washing his godlike body. Come on, Annie, get on with it! What's stopping you?'

I hesitated, standing there in my corsets and petticoat, to undress completely in front of Marthe ... She stared at me as if at some rare animal.

'O Annie, saintly Annie, are there two mugs in the world like you? I'll turn my back, then you can scrub your fair body in peace.'

She went over to the window. But the room itself embarrassed me and I could see myself in the glass, long and brown like a date ... Suddenly, Marthe shamelessly turned round. I shrieked, I plastered my arms against my dripping thighs, I contorted myself, I implored her ... Appearing not to hear me, she put up her lorgnette and stared at me curiously.

'Funny creature! It's obvious you're not from these parts. You look like one of those females in an Egyptian mosaic ... or a serpent standing on its tail or a slender brownstone jar ... Staggering! Annie, you'll never convince me your mother didn't have an affair with a donkey-boy in the shade of the Pyramids.'

'Marthe, *please*! You know perfectly well how that kind of joke shocks me ...'

'I'm quite aware of it. Here catch your chemise, you great silly! At your age, behaving like a prudish schoolgirl! ... *I'd* go stark naked in front of three thousand people, if it was the fashion. To think one always hides one's best features!'

'Does one? Madame Chessenet certainly wouldn't agree with you.'

'What perspicacity! (You don't like her, do you? that amuses me.) She must have breasts she could wear as the very last word in fashion, as a flat stole with the end coming down to her knees.'

Her chattering presence acted as a tonic on my laziness and ended by overcoming my childish prudery. Moreover, Marthe has the gift of making one forgive her almost anything.

While I was arranging my white tulle jabot in front of the glass, Marthe leant out of the window and described what was going on under her eyes.

'I can see Léon searching for us, looking exactly like a lost poodle ... He thinks we've gone to listen to the music. Good riddance!'

'Why?'

'For fear he should bore me, of course! I can see a staggering lady, dressed from head to foot in real Valenciennes, but with a mug as wrinkled as a withered greengage ... I can see the idiotic backs of men in dented panamas that look like squashed meringues ... I can see ... Aha!'

'What is it?'

'Hi! Hi! All right, nothing to be alarmed about! Yes, yes, it's us, come up!'

'You're crazy, Marthe! Everyone's staring at you. Who are you talking to?'

'The little Van Langendonck.'

'Calliope?'

'None other!'

'Is she here?'

'Presumably, since I'm calling out to her.'

I frowned involuntarily; still another connexion Alain would like to break off and which he keeps as distant as possible. Not that this little Cypriot, the widow of a Walloon, gets herself talked about as much as Chessenet, but my husband objects to her flamboyant, languorous beauty which offends his sense of good taste. I had not realized that there was a code of strict conventions for beauty, but Alain assures me there is.

Calliope Van Langendonck, known as 'the violet-eyed Goddess', announced her arrival by an elegant rustle of silks, made an effective theatrical entrance, overwhelmed Marthe with kisses, exclamations, trailing laces, and lapis-lazuli glances veiled by eyelids armed with lashes that glittered like lances, then flung herself on me. I was ashamed of feeling so stiff and unresponsive, so I offered her a chair. Marthe was already bombarding her with questions:

'Calliope, which is the lucky vessel you've got in tow here this year?'

'*Qu'est-ce*, vessel? ... Oh, yes ... No vessel, I am by mine own self.'

She frequently repeats what one has just said with a charming, puzzled air of listening to herself and mentally translating. Is it coquetry or a ruse to give herself time to choose her reply?

I remember, last winter, she was mixing up Greek, Italian, English, and French with an ingenuousness too overdone to be sincere. Her 'babelism', as Claudine, who finds her wildly amusing, calls it, and her carefully cultivated gibberish, attract attention like an additional charm.

'Alone? Tell that to the marines.'

58

'But it is true. One must take care, two months each *anno*, to keep looks.'

'It's worked very well up to now, hasn't it, Annie?'

'Oh, yes. You've never looked prettier, Calliope. The Arriège waters obviously do you good.'

'The waters? I take *jamais* . . . never . .'

'Then, why . . .?'

'Because the altitude's excellent here and I meet people I know and I can dress economically.'

'Admirable woman! All the same, sulphur's good for the skin, isn't it?'

'No, it's *kakon* . . . bad for skin. I take care skin with a special recipe – Turkish.'

'Tell us quick. I'm panting with excitement and I'm sure Annie hasn't a dry stitch on her.'

Calliope, who has left practically all her definite and indefinite articles behind in the isle of Cyprus, spread out her glittering hands magisterially.

'You take . . . old glove buttons, mother-of-pearl, you put in *avothiki* . . . egg-cup . . . and you squeeze lemon quite whole over . . . The next day, she's paste . . .'

'Who's *she*?'

'The buttons and the lemon. And you spread on face and you are whiter than, whiter than . . .'

'Don't bother to find the word. Thanks immensely, Calliope.'

'I can *ancora* give recipe for removing spots woollens . . .'

'No, that's enough, good Lord! Not all the same day! How long have you been in Arriège?'

'One, *due, trois* . . . seven days . . . I'm so happy to see you! I want not to leave you again. When you suddenly called from the *fen* . . . window, I had *spavento* and I dropped my sunshade!'

I was disarmed. Alain himself could not have kept a

straight face under this flood of crazy polyglottism. If this frivolous creature can make the long hours of my 'season' seem shorter, I'll see her as much as she likes, in Arriège.

What need had Marthe to drag me round that bandstand ? I came back with a splitting migraine and feeling as if my skin bore the almost physical imprint of all those stares directed at us. Those people, the bathers and water-drinkers of Arriège, stripped us and devoured us with their cannibal eyes. I feel sick with apprehension at the thought of all the tittle-tattle and spying and scandal-mongering going on among these people with nothing to do and riddled with boredom. Luckily, very few faces I knew except the little Van Langendonck. Renaud and Claudine arrive in three days' time; they've booked their suite.

What a dreary bedroom this is ! The harsh electric light glares down from the ceiling on my dead, empty bed ... I feel lonely, lonely to the point of weeping, so lonely that I made Léonie stay and take down my hair so as to have a familiar presence with me as long as possible ... Come, my black Toby – warm, silent little dog who adores my very shadow – come and lie at my feet. Your sleep is feverish after the long journey, agitated by simple straightforward nightmares ... Perhaps you're dreaming that we're being separated again ?

Don't be frightened, Toby. At this moment, the severe master is asleep on the colourless ocean, for his bed-time is as carefully regulated as all the rest of his life ... He has wound up his watch, he has laid his tall white body, cold from the icy tub, between the sheets. Is he dreaming of Annie ? Will he sigh in the night, will he wake up in the blackness, the deep blackness that his dilated pupils will pattern with gold half-moons and processions of roses? Suppose, at that very minute, he were calling his docile Annie, searching for her smell of roses and white carnations with the tortured smile of an Alain I have only seen and possessed in dreams? No. I would have felt it through the air, over all those miles of distance...

Let's go to bed, my little black dog. Marthe is playing baccarat.

My dear Alain,

I am getting used to this hotel life. It's an effort I hope you'll put down to my credit, just as I give you credit for every victory gained over my apathy.

All the same, the days are longer for me than for the people who are taking the cure. Marthe, valiant as usual, is submitting herself to a very severe régime of douches and massage. Léon only drinks the waters; I just look on.

We've met Madame Van Langendonck who is here on her own. Believe me, dear Alain, I did not in any way seek this meeting. Marthe is only being affable to her and says that watering-place friendships are the easiest things in the world to break off in Paris. So I hope you are reassured that our relations are purely superficial. Besides, she is staying at the Casino and we are at the Grand-Hotel

I also believe the Renaud — Claudine couple will be arriving in a few days. It will be almost impossible for us to avoid seeing them; in any case I get the impression that you consider the husband acceptable socially because he knows everyone. As to his wife, we shall deal with the situation as best we can. For that I rely on Marthe, who has acquired from you some of your unerring sense of the right thing to do on any occasion.

I am writing only about Marthe and myself, dear Alain. You have forbidden me to pester you with my solitude, useless but so well-intentioned! So now you shall also be told that we get up at quarter-to-seven, and that on the stroke of seven we are sitting at little tables in the dairy. A glass of warm, frothy milk is put in front of us and we drink it slowly, watching the sun suck up the morning mist.

We have to breakfast as early as seven because the medicinal baths are at ten. People arrive in dressing-gowns without even taking time to make the most cursory toilet. This early rising is not becoming to all the women and I admire Marthe for surviving the ordeal so well. She appears swathed in linens and muslins, wearing snowy frilled caps in which she looks charming.

Your Annie does not deploy so much art. She turns up in a tailored skirt and a soft silk blouse, and the absence of corsets makes not the slightest difference to my waistline. My night plait is tied up in a 'door-knocker' with a white ribbon and I wear a cloche hat of woven straw. Not an outfit to cause a sensation!

After two cups of milk and as many little croissants, a walk in the park, then back to the hotel to see if there are any letters and to get properly dressed. At ten o'clock, Marthe disappears to her douche and I am left alone till midday. I stroll, I read, I write to you. I try to imagine your life, your cabin, the smell of the sea, the throbbing of the screw . . .

Good-bye, dear Alain, take good care of yourself and of your affection for

Annie

That was all I could find to write to him. I broke off a dozen times, some clumsiness on the verge of dropping from my pen. What evil spirit inhabits me, so that I am already writing 'clumsiness' where the word ought to be 'frankness'?

But could I write everything? I dread my husband's anger, even at a distance, if I had told him that I live in the constant company of Calliope, and of Maugis who arrived three days ago and never leaves us . . . The ten-five train tomorrow brings Claudine and her husband . . . Like a coward, I tell myself that a complete confession when Alain returns will earn me no more than a serious sermon. He won't have seen Calliope in the dairy in the morning in 'wanton disarray' – so disarrayed and so wanton that I turn my eyes away when I talk to her. Clouds of tulle that keep slipping down, flounced négligés yawning wide open over the golden skin and extraordinary lace mantillas to veil her dishevelled hair. Yesterday morning, however, she turned up in a vast dust-coat of silvery glacé silk, so hermetic and so decent that I was amazed. All round us, the panamas and the check caps were regretfully searching for glimpses of amber skin.

I complimented her on her correct attire. She burst into her ear-splitting laugh and shrieked: 'Oh this thing! I had to wear it! I haven't a stitch on underneath!'

I didn't know where to look. All the caps and panamas had bent towards her, with an automatic jerk, like puppets bowing . . .

Luckily, Calliope is alone. Alone? Hmm! Sometimes, when we are walking together, we run into extremely presentable gentlemen who swerve aside with rather too much affected discretion, rather too much sublime indifference. She sweeps past them, her small figure stiffly upright, with a fan-like flutter of her eyelids which she has tried unsuccessfully to teach me.

The hour of the sulphur bath draws us together by creating a desert all round us. Léon, extremely depressed these days, often comes and sits at our table and risks startling ties and vivid waistcoats that suit his ivory complexion. He goes off every quarter of an hour to drink one of the four glasses of the water. He is trying hard to make an impression on Calliope and keeps paying her literary compliments.

To my great astonishment she receives his advances with barely-concealed disdain and a cold, lofty blue stare which implies:

'What does this slave want?'

There is also ... Marthe. Yes, Marthe. I hesitate even to write it ... That Maugis dogs her heels far too closely and she endures his presence as if she were unaware of it. I cannot believe it. Marthe's glittering eyes see everything, hear everything, pounce on the thought behind the eyes they look into. How is it she doesn't tear that delicate, dimpled little hand of hers away from the lips of that creature that say a prolonged good morning and good night to it twice a day? Maugis reeks of alcohol. He is intelligent, yes, and extremely well-informed under all his half-drivelling banter; Alain tells me he is a redoubtable swordsman and that absinthe has not yet made his wrist tremble. But ... ugh!

She's just amusing herself – that's what I'd like to hope. She's flirting for the pleasure of seeing her adorer's glorious eyes become bloodshot and yearning when they look at her. She's just amusing herself ...

I've just come back from accompanying Marthe to her douche. I am still shaken by the experience.

In a hideous rough pine cabin, dripping on every wall and impregnated with sulphur and steam, I assisted, behind a wooden screen, at the nameless torture this douche-massage is. In a flash, Marthe was naked. I blinked at so much shamelessness and so much whiteness. Marthe is white, like Alain, with more pink underneath. Without a flicker of embarrassment she turned a pair of impudent, deeply-dimpled buttocks towards me while she strapped a rubber cap round her temples, a revolting head-dress that made her look like a fishwife.

Then she swung round ... and I was struck dumb by the character this pretty woman's face assumed, deprived of its wavy hair: eyes so piercing they looked almost maniacal, a short, solid jaw, a coarsely-modelled ruthless brow, I searched in vain for the Marthe I knew in this one who frightened me. This disturbing face was laughing above a plump, dainty, almost too feminine body, all exaggerated taperings and exaggerated curves ...

'Hi, Annie, are you falling asleep on your feet?'

'No. But I've had quite enough already. This cabin, that rubber cap ...'

'I say, Catherine, shall we see if she's a brave girl, this little sister-in-law of mine? What about the two of us giving her a good douche, with the full jet on?'

I looked apprehensively at the sexless creature in an oilcloth apron, perched on a pair of wooden clogs. She laughed, displaying red gums.

'If Madame will kindly lie down ... we've lost quite a bit of your fifteen minutes ...'

'I'm coming, I'm coming.'

With a bound, Marthe cleared the edge of a kind of sloping open coffin I had not noticed before and lay down, her hands over breasts to protect them from too rude a shock. The daylight from above lit up the veins in her skin, sculptured the fine creases, harshly illuminated all the red gold fuzz with which her body was fleeced. I blushed in the shadow. I could never have believed Marthe was so hairy ... I blushed even more at the thought that Alain's body was covered with the same reddish-gold fuzz, like fine copper wire. Marthe waited with her eyes closed and her elbows trembling, then the sexless creature aimed two great rubber hoses that hung from the ceiling at her.

There was an outburst of piercing shrieks and imploring supplications. Under the cold jet, thicker than my wrist, Marthe twisted herself like a severed caterpillar, sobbed, ground her teeth and swore. When the hot jet succeeded the cold one, she sighed, appeased and comforted.

The creature douched with one hand and with the other great solid hand kept remorselessly slapping the delicate body that was now marbled with fiery red.

After five minutes of this appalling torture, a big warmed towel-robe, a dry friction, and Marthe, delivered of the revolting rubber cap, was looking at me, still breathless and panting, with big tears in the corner of her eyes.

In a choked voice, I asked her if it was like that every morning.

'Every single one, my child. As Claudine remarked last year: "Apart from an earthquake, they haven't found a more effective method of stimulating the circulation."'

'Oh, Marthe, it's atrocious! that jet's more brutal than any bludgeon ... it made you cry and sob ... The whole thing's too horrible!'

Already half-dressed, she gave me a curious, one-sided smile; her nostrils were still quivering.

'I don't find it so,' she said.

Meals here are a torture to me. We have a choice between two restaurants, both of which are attached to the Casino, for the hotels serve no meals and Arriège is a town only in name, since it consists entirely of the Casino, the thermal establishment, and four big hotels. These refectories, where we present ourselves like boarding-school pupils or prisoners, where at midday one is roasted by the harsh mountain sun, are enough to destroy my appetite entirely. I thought of having meals sent up to

66

my room but all they would bring me would be warmed-up left-overs, and besides, it would be unkind to Marthe for whom meals are a pretext for tattling and poking one's nose into other people's affairs . . . I'm beginning to talk like Marthe myself!

Calliope always sits at our table and so does Maugis to whom I find it hard to be civil. Marthe devotes her attention to him, appears to be interested in his critical articles and tries to coax, or rather bully, him into doing one on *The Tragic Hearts*, my brother-in-law's latest novel, to whip up the sales and to publicize water-places . . .

Léon devours the tough meat with an anaemic man's appetite and goes on paying assiduous court to Calliope who persists in sending him back to his sixty lines with the contempt of a royal princess for a paid scribe. Funny little woman! I have to admit it is I who seek her out now. She talks about herself with embarrassed volubility, fishing in some foreign language for the word she lacks in ours, and I listen to the jerky narrative of her life as if it were a fairy story.

I forget myself in listening to her — most of all while Marthe is having her douche, at the hour when the place is deserted. I sit opposite her in a big wicker armchair, behind the dairy, and, while she talks, I admire her adorned and disarrayed beauty.

'When I was little,' Calliope said one morning, 'I was very beautiful.'

'Why, "I *was*"?'

'*Parce que* I am less. The old woman who did our washing always used to spit in my face.'

'The disgusting creature! Didn't your parents sack her?'

Calliope's lovely blue eyes enveloped me in disdain.

'Sack her? In my country old women must spit on

pretty little girls, saying "Phtu! Phtu!". It's to keep beautiful and guard against evil eye. I was kept *kallista* too on account my mother, the day I baptized, had meal put on table at night.'

'Oh?'

'Yes. You put many things to eat on table and you go to bed. Then the *mires* come.'

'Who?'

'The *mires*. You don't see them but they come to eat. And you put each *chaise*, *chiesa*, how you say? chair, right against wall because if one of the *mires* bumped her elbow in passing to *s'asseoir* at table, she would give ... bad spell on little child.'

'How charming these old customs are! The *mires*, as you call them, are they fairies?'

'Fairies? I do not know. They're *mires* ... Oh dear, I've got a headache.'

'Would you like some aspirin? I've got some in my room.'

Calliope ran a hand with rose-tinted nails over her smooth forehead.

'No, thank you. It's my own fault. I not made the crosses.'

'What crosses?'

'Like this, on the pillow.'

With the flat of her hand, she traced a series of hurried little crosses on her knee.

'You make the little crosses and quick, quick you lay your head on the place and the bad visitors doesn't come in sleep nor *mal-de-tête* nor anything.'

'You're sure?'

Calliope shrugged her shoulders and stood up.

'Of course I'm sure. But you ... you is a people without religion.'

'Where are you running off to, Calliope?'

'It's *devtera* ... Monday. I must do my nails. Here's something again you not know! Do the nails Monday, health. Do the nails Tuesday, wealth.'

'And you prefer health to wealth? How I agree with you!'

She was already walking away but she turned round, clutching armfuls of her dishevelled laces.

'I not prefer ... Monday I do one hand, and Tuesday the other.'

Between noon and five o'clock an inhuman heat prostrates all the bathers. The majority shut themselves up in the huge vestibule of the Casino which looks like a waiting-room in some modern station. Lying back in rocking-chairs, they flirt – poor wretches! – they suck iced coffee and doze to the sound of an orchestra as drowsy as themselves. I often absent myself from these predictable pleasures, embarrassed by people's stares, by Maugis' ill manners, by the noise of some thirty children and their already affected unselfconsciousness.

For I have seen little girls of thirteen there, already developing a woman's calves and hips, shamelessly exploiting the so-called privileges of childhood. Straddled over the leg of a grown-up male cousin or perched on a bar-stool with her knees up to her chin, one adorable little blonde with knowing eyes shows all she can of herself and studies the shamefaced excitement of the men with an icy, catlike gaze. Her mother, a fat, blotchy-faced cook, says ecstatically: 'What a baby she is for her age!' I cannot run into this impudent brat without feeling uncomfortable. She has invented a game of blowing soap-bubbles and chasing them with a woollen racquet. Now males of all ages blow into clay pipes and run after soap-bubbles so as to brush against the little girl, steal her pipe, and snatch her away with one arm when she leans out of the bay window. Oh, what a vile beast must lie dormant in certain men !

Thank heaven, there still remain some real babies, little boys with bare cigar-brown calves and the clumsy charm of bear-cubs; little girls growing too fast, all angles and long thin feet; tiny tots with arms like pink sausages, dented with soft creases as if they had been tied up with string – like that fat little cherub of four, who had had an accident in his first knickerbockers, and who whispered, very red in the face, to his severe and disgusted English governess: 'Does ev'yone know I've been in my trousers?'

Today, I slipped away after lunch and went back to the hotel. I crossed the dangerous tract of sunlight that separates it from the Casino. For twenty-five seconds I savoured the scorching pleasure of feeling as if I were being swept off my feet by the blast of heat; my back sizzled and my ears buzzed. On the verge of falling, I took refuge in the cool darkness of the lobby where a smell of old casks came up through an open door leading down to the cellars, a smell of red wine turning to vinegar. Then I was back in my silent room that already smells of my scent, back on the less hostile bed where I flung myself in my chemise to lie there half-undressed and daydream till five o'clock.

Toby lightly licked my bare feet with a hot, red tongue, then fell prone on the carpet. But this caress not only gave me gooseflesh; it left me shuddering as if I had been outraged and switched my thoughts on to a dangerous path . . . My semi-nakedness reminded me of Marthe's douche, of what she was seeking in those jets that buffeted her, of the whiteness of my husband's – my dream husband's – body . . . To free myself from the obsession – was it really to free myself? . . . . I jumped out

70

of bed and ran to look for Alain's latest photograph that I had hidden between two sachets.

Whatever had happened ? ... Was I actually dreaming ? I could not recognize that handsome young man there ... Those harsh eyebrows, that arrogant stance like a cock ! No, surely I was mistaken ... or perhaps the photographer had absurdly overdone the re-touching ?

But no, that man there was my husband who is far away at sea. I trembled before his picture as I tremble before himself. A slavish creature, unconscious of its chains – that is what he has made of me ... Shattered, I searched obstinately for one memory in our past as a young married couple that could delude me again, that could give me back the husband I *believed* I had. Nothing, I could find nothing – only my whipped child's submissiveness, only his cold condescending smile.

I wish I knew I were delirious, or dreaming. Ah ! the cruel, cruel man ! When did he hurt me most deeply ... when he left me and sailed away – or the very first time he spoke to me ?

FIVE

WE were waiting, behind closed shutters, in Marthe's bedroom which is bigger than mine for Claudine and Calliope who were coming to tea. Claudine had arrived last night with her husband and was making an exception and coming alone as Marthe was excluding men today 'to give herself a rest'. By way of resting, she was pacing round the room; even when she stopped for a moment, she did not stand still but shifted impatiently from one foot to another like a soldier marking time. She was wearing a green muslin dress – a harsh, impossible green that exaggerated the whiteness of her skin and kindled her tempestuous hair to a blaze. Into its low neckline, she had tucked a great pink richly-scented common rose. Marthe has an infallible eye for violent, yet successful, colour contrasts in the things she wears.

She was obviously extremely agitated: her eyes were menacing and her mouth unsmiling. Finally she sat down, did some rapid scribbling on a sheet of paper and muttered some figures.

'It's two louis a day here ... fifteen hundred francs due to Hunt when we get back ... and that fool who wants us to take in Bayreuth on the way ... Life's somewhat complicated!'

'Are you talking to me, Marthe?'

'I'm talking to you and not talking to you, I'm saying that life is complicated.'

'Complicated ... very, in some ways.'

'Exactly. "Very, in some ways." Suppose you had to find five hundred louis?'

'Five hundred louis?'

'Don't wear yourself out making calculations ... it comes to ten thousand francs. If you'd got to produce them out of a hat in three weeks from now, what would you do?'

'I ... I should write to the bank manager ... and to Alain.'

'How simple!'

She sounded so acid that I was afraid I had offended her.

'Why did you say it so bitterly, Marthe? ... Is it ... is it because you need money?'

Her hard grey eyes softened:

'My poor innocent child, you distress me. Of course I need money ... All the time, all the time!'

'But, Marthe, I thought you and Léon were well-off. His novels sell, and there's your dowry ...'

'Yes, yes. But one's got to eat. Porterhouse steak costs the earth this year. All in all, we've only thirty thousand francs a year – to cover everything. Do you imagine a woman can live decently on that unless she's a dim little moth?'

I looked thoughtful for a moment to give the impression of making calculations.

'Well ... perhaps it is rather a tight squeeze. But, Marthe, why on earth didn't you ...?'

'Didn't I what?'

'Come to me. *I've* got some money and I'd be only too pleased ...'

She kissed me – a kiss that sounded like a slap – and pulled my ear.

'You're sweet. I'm not saying no. But not now. Leave it for the moment, I've still got one or two strings to pull that haven't been overworked. I'll keep you as the last resort. Besides it amuses me, fighting against money

– waking up and finding a bill that's come in for the tenth time with "urgent" on it and staring at my empty hands and telling myself: "Tonight there have got to be twenty-five louis in that little fist."'

I stared flabbergasted at her – at this diminutive Bellona in a grasshopper-green dress. 'Fight ... struggle ...' the alarming words conjured up images of murderous gestures, tensed muscles, blood-stained victories ... I sat there as if paralysed, my hands inert, gazing at her and thinking of my recent tears over Alain's photograph, of my crushed, ineffective life ... Then a thought suddenly disturbed my inertia.

'Marthe ... how do you manage?'

'What d'you mean?'

'How do you manage, when you need money so badly?'

She smiled, averted her head, then looked at me again with a sweet, far-away expression.

'All right, I'll tell you ... I touch Léon's publisher ... I get round the tailor, or else I terrorize him ... And besides, now and then, I get unexpected repayments ...'

'You mean money you were owed ... that you'd lent to people?'

'Something of the kind ... I can hear Claudine. Who's she talking to?' She opened the door and leant out into the corridor. I followed her with my eyes, painfully aware of having dissembled. For the first time, I had just feigned ignorance and pretended to be as idiotically naïve as the Cabbage-Rose. 'Unexpected repayments! ...' Marthe troubles me.

Claudine was certainly talking in the corridor. I could hear her saying gutturally, 'My girrrl ...' What girl? And why with such a tender voice?

She appeared, holding her Fanchette on a lead. The

cat minced in with a calm, undulating gait, but its green eyes blackened at the sight of us. Marthe, in raptures, clapped her hands as if she were at the theatre.

'What a marvellous idea, Claudine! Where did you get that delicious animal? At Barnum's?'

'Certainly not. At home. In Montigny. Sit, Fanchette.'

Claudine removed her boy's hat and shook out her curls. I find that ivory skin and that fierce, yet sweet expression of hers extraordinarily attractive. Her cat sat down primly with her tail wrapped round her front paws. It was a good thing I had sent Toby out for a walk with Léonie; she would have scratched him.

'Hullo, you, princess in the tower.'

'Hullo, Claudine. Did you have a good journey?'

'Very good. Renaud charming. He flirted with me all the time, so ardently that I didn't feel for one minute as if we were married ... Would you believe it ... a man wanted to buy Fanchette from me? I gave him a look as if he'd raped my mother ... It's hot in here. Are there a lot of ladies coming?'

'No, no, only Calliope Van Langendonck.'

Claudine nimbly swung her foot over a chair – a very high chair.

'What luck! I adore Calliope. Trireme ahoy! She'll keep us in fits. Besides which, she's pretty and she's the last reincarnation of the "soul of antiquity".'

'What nonsense!' exclaimed Marthe. 'Why she's as cosmopolitan as a croupier in a casino!'

'That's what I meant. In my over-simple imagination she's the living embodiment of all those people down below us.'

'The moles?' I chaffed her, shyly.

'No, you sly little bitch. Down below ... on the map. Here she is! Appear, Calliope, Hebe, Aphrodite, Mnasidika ... I'm trotting out all my Greek for you!'

Calliope gave the impression of being naked in a too-sumptuous dress of black Chantilly lace over flesh-coloured crêpe-de-Chine. She almost collapsed on the threshold.

'I'm dead ... three flights ...'

'Is bad for the skin,' Claudine finished for her.

'But is good for pregnant woman. It makes child drop.'

MARTHE (*horrified*) Are you pregnant, Calliope?

CALLIOPE (*serene*) No ... *jamais*, never.

MARTHE (*bitter*) You're lucky. Neither am I, as it happens. But what a ghastly bore it is, having to take all these precautions. How do *you* prevent it?

CALLIOPE (*modest*) I am a widow.

CLAUDINE Obviously, that's one method. But not inevitably sufficient in itself. What did you do when you weren't a widow?

CALLIOPE I made crosses on, before. And I cough, after.

MARTHE (*bursting with laughter*) Crosses! ... On which of you? You or your partner?

CALLIOPE On both, *chérie*.

CLAUDINE Ah! Ah! And you coughed afterwards? Is that the Greek rite?

CALLIOPE No. You cough like this (*coughing*) and it's gone.

MARTHE (*dubious*) It gets in quicker than it gets out ... Claudine, just pass me the peach salad ...

CLAUDINE (*absorbed*) No one could call me curious, but I would like to have seen his face ...

CALLIOPE Whose face?

CLAUDINE The face of the late Van Langendonck when you were 'making crosses over'.

CALLIOPE (*candid*) But I didn't make them on face!

CLAUDINE (*unable to control herself*) Oh, this is bliss!

(suffocating with laughter) Calliope ... you incredible woman ... you'll make me choke to death in a moment ...

She shrieked and doubled herself up with delight; Marthe too was convulsed with laughter. In spite of being shocked and disgusted by them, I could not help smiling in the dimness that protected me. But it did not protect me enough; Claudine had noticed the silent amusement for which I rebuked myself sternly.

'Aha! Saint Annie, I saw you! Run away and play in the park at once or else don't look as if you understood. No, on second thoughts, smile again! (Her harsh voice had suddenly become gentle and sing-song.) 'When the corners of your mouth go up, your eyelids come down. Your smile is far more ambiguous than Calliope's stories, little Annie ...'

Marthe thrust the screen of an open fan between Claudine and myself.

'If you go on like this, you'll be calling my sister-in-law "Rézi" in a minute! Thanks, I don't want that sort of thing going on in my respectable bedroom!'

Rézi? Whatever did that mean? I plucked up my courage.

'You said ... "Rézi"? Is that a word in a foreign language?'

'You couldn't have put it better!' retorted Claudine, while Marthe and Calliope exchanged knowing smiles. Then, all at once, her gaiety vanished. She stopped sucking her iced coffee through a straw, and fell into a momentary day-dream. Her darkened eyes looked exactly like the eyes of her white cat who was staring pensively into space, as if at some invisible menace ...

What else did they say? I can't remember much ... I

withdrew further and further into the shadow of the shutters. I daren't write down the scraps I do remember. All sorts of horrors! Calliope retailed them quite naturally, with an exotic shamelessness; Marthe, crudely and bluntly; Claudine with a kind of languid ferocity I found less revolting.

Finally they began to question me, with much laughter about gestures and positions, about things I daren't name even to myself. I didn't understand everything, I stammered and pulled my hands away; in the end they let me alone, though Claudine murmured, looking deep into my pale eyes that are too receptive to other people's will: 'This Annie of ours – she's as engaging as a young girl.' She was the first to leave, leading her white cat with its green collar and yawning in our faces: 'It's too long since I've seen my great man; time's beginning to pall on me!'

Maugis 'sticks' closer and closer. He incenses Marthe with his homage which rises up in fumes of whisky. These meetings at the five o'clock concerts put me out of all patience. Calliope is invariably there, surrounded by men staring at her like a pack of hounds and the Renaud – Claudine couple, amorous and irritating. Yes, irritating! The way they smile into each other's eyes and sit knee to knee, as if they'd only been married a fortnight! Besides, *I* have seen people married a fortnight who didn't behave in a way that attracted attention.

I remember a very recently-married couple dining at a small table in a restaurant; he red-haired, she exaggeratedly dark, whose faces never betrayed desire, whose hands never touched, whose feet never met under the tent of tablecloth ... Often she would droop her eyelids over her transparent eyes 'the colour of wild chicory flowers', she would pick up her fork and put it down again, cool her hand against the beaded side of the water-jug like a fever-patient grown used to fever. *He* ate with an appetite as healthy as his teeth and spoke in an authoritative voice: 'Annie, you're wrong; this meat isn't underdone. It's exactly the right degree of rareness ∴..' So blind, so indifferent, he was unaware of that sweet fever, he did not even see those too-heavy lashes veiling the blue eyes. He never guessed my anguish nor how I was longing for, yet dreading, the moment that had not yet come when my pleasure would respond to his ... How painful it is even to write this ... It was always the same ... I yielded myself, frightened and obedient, to his simple, robust caress which broke off too soon, at the instant when, rigid and choking back tears, I thought I must be on the brink of death itself, when my whole being was crying out for and expecting ... I did not know what.

I know now. Boredom, loneliness, an afternoon of atrocious migraine and ether have turned me into a sinner full of remorse. A sin which is always threatening me and against which I struggle desperately ... Ever since I took to writing this diary, I can see myself emerging a little more clearly every day, like a blackened portrait being cleaned by an expert hand. How did Alain, who was so little concerned about my moral miseries, guess what had happened between me and ... Annie? I have no idea. Perhaps the jealousy of a betrayed animal illuminated him that day ...

What is it that has suddenly made me see clearly? His absence? Have a few hundred miles of land and water worked this miracle? Or have I perhaps drunk the philtre that restored Siegfried's memory to him? But the philtre also restored his love, and, in my case, alas! ... What have I to cling to now? All the people about me are speeding and striving towards the goal

of their life ... Marthe and Léon are toiling with all
their might, he for big editions, she for luxury. Claudine
loves and Calliope permits herself to be loved ... Maugis
intoxicates himself – Alain fills his life with a thousand
exacting vanities: respectability; cutting a brilliant, but
eminently correct figure in society; the necessity of living in a well-ordered house, of weeding out his address-
book as one weeds out servants' references, of training
his wife whom he rides on too short a rein like his half-
bred English horse ... They go about, they do things,
and *I* stay here, listless and empty-handed ...

Marthe burst in in the middle of this fit of black
depression. She herself seemed less cheerful than usual,
or else less valiant, and her red mobile mouth drooped
at the corners, even when she laughed. But perhaps it
was I who was seeing everything warped?

She sat down without looking at me, arranged the
folds of a lace skirt that she wore under a little
eighteenth-century jacket of stiff Chinese silk. White
plumes quivered in her hat. I don't much care for that
costume – it's too elaborate, too suggestive of a society
wedding. Secretly I prefer my own ivory voile dress with
fine tucking everywhere, on the yoke, above the flounce
of the skirt, at the top of the sleeves that flare out below
it in wings ...

'Are you coming?' demanded Marthe brusquely.

'Coming where?'

'Oh, why must you always look as if you'd just dropped from the moon? To the music ... it's five o'clock.'

'The fact is I ...'

Her gesture cut me short.

'No, spare me that! You've said it already. Get your
hat on and let's be off.'

Normally I would have obeyed, half-unconsciously.

But today had been a troubled day and it had changed me.

'No, Marthe, I assure you, I *have* got a headache.'

She wriggled her shoulders impatiently.

'Yes, I know. The air will do you good. Come along.'

Gently, I continued to say no. She bit her lips and her red, brown-pencilled eyebrows drew together in a frown.

'Look here, Annie. The fact is I need you – there!'

'Need me?'

'Yes, need you. I don't want to be alone ... with Maugis.'

'Alone with Maugis? You must be joking. There'll be Claudine and Renaud and Calliope.'

Marthe fidgeted and turned a little pale; her hands were trembling.

'I implore you, Annie – don't make me lose my temper.'

Taken aback, but defiant, I remained seated. She did not look at me but spoke, with her eyes staring at the window.

'I ... I *particularly* need you to come because ... because Léon is jealous.'

She was lying. I could feel she was lying. She guessed it and, at last, turned her blazing eyes on me.

'Yes, all right, it's a fib. I want to talk to Maugis without anyone seeing us. I need you to make the others believe you're accompanying him and me a little way up the path ... thirty paces behind like an English governess. You can take a book or a piece of needlework or anything you fancy. There! Got it? What's your answer? Will you do me this small favour?'

I blushed for her. With Maugis! And she had counted on me ... for ... oh, no!

As I shook my head, she gave me a furious stamp.

'Idiot! Do you imagine I'm going to sleep with him in a ditch in the park? Get it into your head that everything's gone wrong, that I can't lay my hands on a penny, that I've got to get, not just one article on Léon's novel that's coming out in October but two articles ... *three* articles ... in the foreign reviews that'll get it sold in London and Vienna! That soak is as tricky as a monkey and we've been pitting our wits against each other for a month, but he'll come across with those articles or I'll ... I'll ...'

She was spluttering with fury, her fist clenched and her face savage. She looked like a stocking-knitter at the foot of the guillotine disguised as an aristocrat. Then, with a magnificent effort, she calmed herself and said coldly,

'That's the situation. Are you coming to the music now? In Paris, I shouldn't be reduced to asking you this. In Paris, a woman with her wits about her can manage these things on her own! But here, in this place where we all live in each other's pockets, where your next-door-neighbour in the hotel counts your dirty nightdresses and the jugs of hot water the maid brings up in the morning ...'

'Just tell me one thing, Marthe ... is it out of love for Léon?'

'Out of love that I'm ... what?'

'Doing all this ... Sacrificing yourself, being friendly with this horrible man ... it's for your husband's glory, isn't it?'

She gave a harsh laugh as she powdered her flaming cheeks.

'All right, if you like, for his glory ... If he's to wear laurels on his brow, he may have to wear something else. You needn't look wildly round for your hat. It's on the bed.'

How much farther are these women going to lead me astray? There is not one of them I wish to resemble! Marthe, who sticks at nothing; Calliope who is as cynical as a harem woman; Claudine who is as unashamed as an animal of all her instincts, even her good ones. Since I can judge them so clearly, heaven preserve me from becoming like any of them!

Yes, I accompanied Marthe to the band-stand, then into the park, with Maugis walking between us. In a deserted path, Marthe said to me casually: 'Annie, your shoelace is coming undone.' Meekly I pretended to re-tie the silk lace, though the knot was perfectly secure, and made no attempt to catch up with them. I walked at some distance behind, my eyes on the ground, not daring to look at their backs and not hearing what they were saying, only a rapid murmur of voices.

When Marthe, excited and triumphant, came to relieve me of my shameful sentry-duty, I heaved a great sigh of relief. She took my arm in a friendly way.

'It's done. Thank you, pet. You've helped me arrange things satisfactorily. But imagine the difficulty! If I'd asked Maugis to meet me alone in the park or the dairy or at one of those little tables where they serve iced coffee, some busybody, male or, worse still, female, would have crashed in on us before we'd been there five minutes. My little game would have been ruined. And seeing him in my room would have been far too risky ...'

'So you're going to get them, Marthe?'

'Get what?'

'The articles in the foreign Reviews.'

'Ah ... yes ... Yes, I'm going to get them and everything else I wanted.'

She was silent for a moment, fluttering her wide sleeves to cool herself. Then she muttered, as if to herself:

'He's rich, the swine.'

I stared at her in amazement.

'Rich? Why should that bother you, Marthe?'

'What I meant by that,' she explained very fast 'is that I envy him for being able to write for his own pleasure instead of slaving away like poor old Léon over there. There he is, as usual, laying siege to Calliope without the faintest success. That Cypriot town has no ramparts but it's amazing how it defends itself!'

'Besides, perhaps the assailant isn't very heavily armed,' I risked shyly.

'Mercy, what next! Annie coming out with improper remarks! I didn't know you were *quite* so well informed about Léon, dear!'

All animation, she rejoined the group of friends we had left. However, I pleaded my migraine again as an excuse to get away and here I am back in my bedroom, with my black Toby at my feet, troubled about myself, dissatisfied with everything, humiliated by the menial service I have just rendered my sister-in-law.

All the things Alain does not suspect! It makes me smile maliciously to think how little he knows about me, even about his favourite sister. I am beginning to hate this Arriège, where my life has been revealed to me with such depressing clarity, where you cannot get away from this restricted little crowd of people who, when you see them so close, seem to be distorted into caricatures of human beings ... I've exhausted any amusement I had in watching these creatures' antics. In the daily procession to the dairy, I see too much plastered-over ugliness in the women's faces, and, in the men's, bestial desires or else utter fatigue. For among them are the sinister faces of the baccarat fiends – drawn and green, with bloodshot eyes. Those faces belong to the numbed bodies of men who have been sitting all night in a chair. As Marthe says, it is not only arthritis that ossifies so many joints here.

I've no longer the least desire to go to the pumproom or to watch Marthe's douche or to gossip in the hall of the casino or to giggle at *Jeanette's Wedding* with Claudine. That perverse creature, who is mad about Debussy, has taken a sadistic fancy to going to the most hackneyed old musical comedies and applauding them frantically. Day after day, at the same hours, the same amusements, the same dressing-up, the same collection of faces . . . I simply cannot stand it any longer. Through the window, my eyes keep straying to the open breach at the western end of the valley – a break in the dark chain that hems us in, a rift of light in which distant mountains, powdered with mother-of-pearl, sparkle against a sky whose pure faint blue is the exact blue of my eyes . . . It is through there now that I can fancy I am escaping . . . Through there I can divine (or only imagine, alas!) another life that will be *my* life, not that broken mechanical doll they call Annie.

My poor black Toby, what am I going to do with you? Now we are going off to Bayreuth! Marthe has decided this with an emphatic authority that spares me any need to argue. All right, Toby, I'll take you with me – it's much the simplest, most honourable thing to do. I promised you I'd keep you, and I need your mute, familiar presence, your short square shadow beside my long one. You loved me enough to respect my sleep, my sadness, my silence, and I love you like a little guardian monster.

I feel young and gay again when I watch you gravely escorting me with your jaw distended by a big green apple that you'll carry about for a whole day, like a precious treasure, or obstinately scratching a pattern on the carpet to try and make it come off. For you live in a state of ingenuous surprise, surrounded by mysteries. The mystery of the coloured flowers on the upholstery of the armchairs; the deceitfulness of the mirrors out of which a phantom bull-terrier glares at you, a black bull-terrier who resembles you like a twin brother; the trap of the rocking-chair that tilts away under your paws . . . *You* don't obstinately try to penetrate the unknown. You growl or else you smile rather sheepishly, and you resume your chewed green apple.

Only two months ago, I too would have said: 'I give up. My master knows how to deal with it.' Now I torment myself and I flee from myself. I flee from myself. Understand what I mean by that please, little dog, full of faith I have lost. It is better, a hundred times better for me to drivel in this diary and to listen to Claudine and Calliope than to linger dangerously alone with myself . . .

Nowadays, we talk of nothing but our going away. Calliope keeps dinning into my ears how heart-broken she is over our departure, larding her laments with constant ejaculations of *'Dio almighty* !' and *'poulaki mou* !'

Claudine observes all this agitation with kindly indifference. Renaud is with her, what does all the rest matter ? Léon, embittered by his failure with Calliope (he cannot forgive her) talks far too much about his novel and about the Bayreuth he means to describe in it – 'a Bayreuth perceived from a particular angle'.

'It's a new subject,' Maugis gravely declared today – Maugis who for ten years has been Bayreuth correspondent to three daily papers.

'It's a new subject when you know how to rejuvenate it,' Léon affirmed pompously. 'Bayreuth seen through the eyes of a woman in love with all her sensual perceptions intensely sharpened by gratified – and illicit! – passion . . . All right, laugh . . . it could make a very good subject and run into twenty editions!'

'At least,' muttered Maugis through a cloud of smoke. 'Anyway, I always agree with the husband of a pretty woman.'

The pretty woman was half-asleep, recumbent in a rocking-chair. Marthe never takes more than a cat-nap.

We were grilling in the park; it was two o'clock, the longest, most stifling hour of the day. The iced coffee was melting in our glasses. I rejoiced in the torrid sun, lying back in a wicker armchair, and I did not even flutter my eyelids – at school they used to call me the lizard . . . Léon kept glancing at his watch, careful not to overstep the time-limit of his recreation. The carcass of Toby, which appeared to be uninhabited, lay prone on the fine sand.

'Are you taking that dog with you?' Marthe sighed faintly.

'Certainly, he's such a well-behaved boy!'

'I don't much care for well-behaved boys, even on railway journeys.'

'Then you can get into another compartment.'

Having made this reply, I marvelled at myself. Last month I should have answered: 'Then I'll get into another compartment.'

Marthe made no comment and appeared to be asleep. After a moment, she opened her vigilant eyes wide.

'I say, you two, don't you think Annie's changed?'

'Hmm . . .' Maugis mumbled, very vaguely.

'Do you think so?' asked Calliope, in a conciliating voice.

'I'm delighted to observe you all agree with me,' mocked my sister-in-law. 'So I shan't surprise you by saying that Annie walks faster, stoops her shoulders less, doesn't keep her eyes always fixed on the ground, and talks almost like a normal human being. Alain's the one who's going to get a surprise !'

Embarrassed, I got up to go.

'It's your activity that galvanizes me, Marthe. Alain won't be so surprised as you think. He always prophesied that you'd have an excellent influence on me. Excuse me, but I'm going indoors to write letters ...'

'I'll come with you,' said Calliope.

She did indeed come with me, without any encouragement on my part. She slipped her dimpled arm under my thin one.

'Annie, I've got a very great favour to ask you.'

Her face was infinitely seductive. Between the sharp-pointed lashes, the lapis-lazuli eyes glittered at me in a suppliant stare, the Cupid's bow mouth was half-open as if on the verge of pouring out the most intimate confidences ... One has to be prepared for anything with Calliope.

'Tell me, dear ... you know if it's anything in my power ...'

When we reached my bedroom, she took my hands with an overdone imitation of an Italian actress.

'Oh, you will, won't you ? You're such a pure ! That's what decided me. *Je suis* ... lost if you refuse me ! But you'll be kind for me ... no ?'

She rolled a little lace handkerchief into a ball and dabbed her eyelashes with it. They were dry. I felt extremely uneasy.

Then she stood very still, fumbling the dozens of curious charms that jingled on her chain (Claudine says Calliope sounds like a little dog when she walks) and staring at the carpet. She seemed to be muttering some-thing to herself.

'It's a prayer to the Moon,' she explained. 'Annie, come to my aid. I need a letter.'

'A letter?'

'Yes. A letter ... *epigraphion*. A good letter, that you'll dictate.'

'But to whom?'

'To ... to ... a very dear friend. A man.'

'Oh!'

Calliope swung up a tragic arm.

'I swear, on oath, on head of my dead parents that he is only Platonic friend!'

I did not answer at once. I wanted to know more.

'But, my dear, why do you need *me* for that?'

She wrung her hands but her face was extremely calm.

'Understand! A very dear friend I love ... Yes, I love him, I swear, Annie! But ... but I not know him too well.'

'Yet you love him!'

'Yes. He wants to marry me. He writes passionate letter and I *réponds* ... answer very little ... because I not know very well how to write.'

'I never heard such nonsense!'

'The truth ... on oath! I speak ... two, t'ree, four, *cinq*, languages, enough to travel with. But I can't write. Especially French ... so complicated if ... if I not find the word ... My friend thinks me ... educated woman, unique, walking encyclopedia ... and I'd so like to appear as he thinks! Otherwise ... as you say in France, don't you? ... the affair's in a cart.'

She looked piteous, she blushed, she twisted her little handkerchief, she turned on all her charm. I asked reflec-tively, in a very chilly voice:

'Tell me, Calliope, whom did you count on before me? After all, I'm presumably not the first ...'

She shrugged her shoulders tempestuously.

'A little boy of my country, who wrote well. He was ... in love with me. And I copied his letters ... but in the other gender of course.'

This calm villainess, instead of arousing my indignation reduced me to helpless laughter. I can't help it, I can't take Calliope seriously, even as a wicked woman. She had completely disarmed me. I opened my blotter.

'Sit down there, Calliope, and we'll try. Although you'll never know how strange it is to me to be writing a love-letter ... Come on. What am I to say?'

'Everything!' she cried with passionate gratitude. 'That I love him! ... That he's far from me! ... that my life has no savour ... that I am fading away ... In fact, all the things one usually says.'

That I love him ... that he is far from me ... I had already treated that theme, but with so little success! Sitting beside Calliope, with my elbows on the table and my eyes on the hand that glittered with rings, I dictated as if in a dream ...

'My beloved friend ...'

'Too cold,' interrupted Calliope. 'I shall write "My soul on the sea!"'

'Just as you like ... "My soul on the sea ..." I can't do it this way, Calliope. Give me the pen ... you can copy it out and alter it afterwards.'

And I wrote feverishly:

'My soul on the sea, you have left me like a house without a master where a forgotten candle still burns. The candle will burn down to the end and passers-by will think the house is inhabited but the flame will burn low in an hour and die out ... unless another hand restores it to glowing life ...'

'Not that, no!' Calliope intervened, leaning over my shoulder. 'Not good, "another hand!" Write "the same hand".'

But I was no longer writing anything. With my head on the table, buried in the crook of my elbow, I was suddenly weeping, furious with myself for being unable to hide my tears ... The game had ended disastrously. Kind little Calliope understood ... not quite correctly ... and overwhelmed me with hugs, with her scent, with condolences and cries of despairing self-reproach:

'Darling! *Psychi mou*! How bad I am! I not think you were all alone! Give me, is finished. I not want more. And, besides, it's enough! The begin, good if I change little. I shall put *palazzo* instead of house and I shall search in French novels for the rest ...'

'Forgive me, Calliope dear. This thundery weather has put my nerves in a wretched state.'

'Nerves! Ah! if women only had nerves!' said Calliope sententiously, rolling her eyes up to the ceiling. 'But ...'

The simple cynical gesture she made completed her sentence so oddly that, in spite of myself, I smiled. She laughed.

'That's so, eh? *Addio, mille remercîments*, and forgive me. I take away beginning of letter. Be with your courage.'

Already outside in the corridor, she reopened the door and thrust her face round it, the face of a mischievous goddess:

'And I'll even copy it twice. Because I have another friend.'

' "Being of a saline and sulphurous nature, the waters of Arrìège are indicated in the case of chronic affections of the skin ..." '

Claudine was reading aloud the little panegyric, bound in an attractive cover, that the thermal establishment provided for the benefit of people taking the cure. We were listening for the last time to the dismal orchestra that always played *fortissimo*, with a rigid strictness of rhythm and not the slightest variation of tone. Between a *Selection from the Dragoons of Villars* and a *March* by Armande de Polignac, Claudine was initiating us, against our will and not without acid comments, into the virtues of the sulphurous spring. Her diction was impeccable, her tone magisterial, her calm imperturbable.

Her white cat, on a lead, was asleep in a wicker chair. 'A chair that costs two sous, like a lady's,' Claudine had insisted. 'Not an iron one because Fanchette feels the cold in her behind!'

'I'm going to play a game!' she cried, suddenly inspired.

'You make me slightly apprehensive,' said her husband with his usual loving glance.

He was smoking fragrant Egyptian cigarettes and sat, for the most part, silent and detached as if he had transferred all his life to the woman he called his 'darling child'.

'A nice party game! I'm going to guess from your faces what diseases you've come here to cure, and, when I make a mistake, I'll pay a forfeit.'

'Pay me one straight away,' cried Marthe. 'I'm as fit as a fiddle.'

'Me too,' growled Maugis, whose face was purple under the panama pulled down as far as his moustache.

'Me too,' said Renaud quietly.

'So am I!' sighed Léon, pale and exhausted.

Claudine, enchantingly pretty in a white straw bonnet, tied under the chin with white tulle strings, menaced us with a pointed finger.

'Attention, all! You're going to see that every one of you has come here for pleasure . . . just like me!'

She picked up her little book again and distributed her diagnoses like so many bouquets.

'Marthe, for you "acne and eczema"! For you, Renaud . . . let's see . . . ah! "furunculosis". Pretty, isn't it? It sounds like the name of a flower. In Annie, I divine "intermittent erysipelas" and in Léon "scrofulous anaemia" . . .'

'He won't thank you much for that,' broke in Renaud who saw a sickly smile on my brother-in-law's face . . .

'And in Maugis . . . Maugis . . . oh, bother, I can't find anything else . . . Ah! I've got it! In Maugis, I diagnose . . . "recurrent pruritus of the genital parts".'

There was an explosion of laughter! Marthe showed all her teeth and impudently directed her laugh straight at the furious Maugis who lifted his panama to pour out a stream of invectives against the brazen hussy. Renaud tried half-heartedly to impose silence, for a respectable group behind us had just taken flight with much scandalized clatter of overturned chairs.

'Pay no attention,' cried Claudine. 'Those people who've gone are just plain jealous,' (she picked up her book again) 'they've only got miserable little diseases not worth having . . . they're just . . . "chronic metritises", petty "aural catarrhs" or miserable twopenny-halfpenny "leucorrheas"!'

'What about you yourself, you poisonous little thing?' burst out Maugis. 'What the hell have you come here for, besides making yourself a thorough pest and disturbing everyone's peace?'

'Hush!' She leant forward, with an impressive mysterious air. 'Don't tell anyone. I've come here for the sake of Fanchette, who suffers from the same complaint as you.'

SIX

BAYREUTH.

Rain. Rain. ... The sky melts into rain, and the sky here is coal-dust. If I lean on the window-sill, my hands and elbows are smeared with black. The same impalpable black powder snows down invisibly on my white serge dress, and if I absent-mindedly stroke my cheek with the palm of my hand I crush a gritty sticky smut into long black streaks. Drops of rain have dried on the flounce of my skirt in little grey spots. Léonie is eternally brushing my clothes and Marthe's. As she does so, she wears a blissful expression that makes her look like a sentimental policeman. It reminds her of her native Saint-Étienne, she declares.

In the west, the sky is turning yellow. Perhaps the rain is going to stop and I shall see Bayreuth otherwise than through this fine, open veil, otherwise too than through the distorting prism of my tears.

For, the moment I arrived, I dissolved into water like the clouds. I feel ashamed to write down the puerile reason for such a crisis of misery, but I will.

At Schnabelweide, where we changed from the Nürnberg-Carlsbad line, the train rushed on in a heedless hurry most untypical of German trains, carrying my trunk and my dressing-case off on their way to Austria. As a result I found myself – after fifteen hours of travelling and sticky all over with this German coal-dust that smells of sulphur and iodoform – without a sponge, without a clean handkerchief, without a comb, in fact without everything absolutely essential. This blow demoralized me, and while Léon and Maugis tore off to the

Information Bureau, I began to cry. I just stood there on the platform, shedding great tears that made little pellets in the dust.

'This Annie of ours was obviously born under Aquarius,' murmured Claudine philosophically.

As a result, my arrival in the 'Holy City' was pitiable and absurd. I was not amused by Marthe's snobbish ecstasies over the postcards, the red glass Grails, the carvings, the plates, and the beer-jugs, all stamped with the image of the god Wagner. Even Claudine, unkempt, with her boater over one ear, hardly raised a smile from me when she brandished a smoking sausage she was clutching triumphantly, right under my nose.

'Look what I've bought!' she cried. 'It's a sort of postman who sells them. Yes, Renaud, a postman! He's got hot sausages in his leather satchel and he fishes them out with a fork, like snakes. You needn't make a face, Marthe, it's delicious! I shall send one to Mélie – I shall tell her it's called a Wagnerwurst . . .'

She went off, dancing, dragging her gentle husband towards a lilac-painted *Konditorei* to eat whipped cream with her sausage . . .

I recovered my luggage, thanks to the zeal of Léon, egged on by Marthe, and the polyglottism of Maugis. The latter speaks as many German dialects as there are tribes in Israel and, with one sentence I found totally intelligible, he galvanized the smiling, apathetic officials into action. I got my own things back at the very moment when Claudine, moved by my plight had just sent me one of her linen chemises . . . so brief, it made me blush . . . and a little pair of Japanese silk knickers patterned with yellow moons. With them was this note: 'Take them, anyway, Annie, if only to dry your tears, and remember I'm a St Martin type. Query: would St Martin have given away his trousers?'

I am waiting, without impatience, for lunchtime, and for the rain to stop. Now and then a rift of blue shows through two heavy sailing clouds, then vanishes. My window looks out on the Opernstrasse, over a boarded footpath that conceals the stagnant water below. The staircase smells of cabbage. My curious coffin-like bed is boxed in during the day under a lid covered with sprigged material. The top sheet buttons on to the eiderdown and my mattress is composed of three pieces, like a Louis XIV chaise longue ... Do I feel the faintest touch of the sacred fever? No, most decidedly no. I envy Marthe who, the moment we arrived at the station, began to sparkle with conversational enthusiasm, already breathing what her husband pompously calls 'the fervour of all the nations who have come to worship the man who was greater than man ...' On the other side of the wall, I can hear that neophyte furiously banging about among her trunks, and emptying the tiny jugs of hot water with a single splash. Léon's voice reaches me only as an inarticulate buzz. Marthe's total silence seems to me ominous. I was not altogether surprised just now when I heard her exclaim in a loud, shrill voice, anything but suggestive of Marie-Antoinette:

'Hell! What a filthy hole!'

Only one pleasurable sensation makes me almost content to sit perfectly still in front of this window, at this rickety little mahogany table: the feeling of being very far away, beyond anyone's reach ... How long is it since Alain went away? A month, a year? I have lost all count of time. I shut my eyes and try to conjure up his fading image; sometimes I strain my ears, as if I thought I heard his footsteps ... Am I awaiting his return or am I dreading it? Often, I turn round sharply with the vivid impression that he is there, that he is going to lay his heavy hand on my shoulder, and my shoulder automatically droops to receive it . . . It is over in a second, but it is like the flash of a danger signal. I know all too well, that if he returned, he would once again be my master. Once again, my neck would bow meekly to the yoke that it has hardly had time to miss. After all, it is as used to wearing it as my hand is to the ring Alain put on it the day we were married, the ring that is a little too tight and has worn a permanent groove in my finger.

For people on a pleasure-trip, how gloomy the three of us were, in that *Restauration* this evening! Certainly the novelty of the place, the feeble, hissing gas-light, the cold wind blowing through the gaps of the tent did not excite me personally to gaiety but I was surprised that Marthe and her husband looked equally lost and constrained. Marthe stared at her chicken and stewed pears on her plate. Léon made notes in a little pocket-book. On what? The place seemed in no way remarkable. This restaurant, the Baierlein, whose vogue is due to its serving meals on a terrace under a striped tent, seemed to me, apart from the stewed pears, much like the one at Arriège. More English women dining there perhaps, and little brown jugs of *Seltzwasser* on the tables. What a lot of English women! Whoever told me they were stiff and reserved? Léon informed me they had come straight from *Parsifal*. Flushed, their hats askew, their admirable hair clumsily twisted up anyhow, they shrieked, wept over their memories of the opera, waved their arms, and never, for a moment, stopped eating. I stared at them – I who was not hungry, who was not weeping, I who was keeping my chilly hands sedately folded inside my wide sleeves – as if they were drunk, wondering half-enviously, half-disgustedly: 'Shall I be like that on Sunday?' To tell the truth, I hope I shall.

Marthe uttered not a word as she studied the diners

97

with her insolent eyes. She must have found their hats unworthy of interest. My brother-in-law went on taking notes. So many notes! People were staring at him. I stared at him too. How extraordinarily French he looked!

In spite of an English tailor, a Swedish bootmaker, and an American hatter, this effeminately handsome man is a supreme example of the French type in all its colourless correctness. I began to wonder what betrayed him at once as a typical average Frenchman, with no great qualities and no great defects. Was it no more than the suavity of his over-frequent gestures and the total lack of character in his regular, well-proportioned features?

Marthe brusquely interrupted my ethnological speculations.

'Please don't talk all at once. Honestly, this place bores me to tears. Isn't there somewhere even *more* giddily exciting?'

'Certainly,' said Léon, consulting his Baedeker. 'The Berlin restaurant. It's smarter, more French, but it has less local colour.'

'I don't care a fig about local colour . . . I've come here for Wagner, not for Bayreuth. All right, let's go to the Berlin tomorrow . . .'

'We shall have to pay ten marks for a *truite au bleu* . . .'

'Why worry? Maugis is good for . . . for standing us a meal . . . maybe a couple . . .'

I decided to intervene.

'But Marthe, *I* feel embarrassed letting Maugis pay for me . . .'

'All right, my dear girl, you can go off by yourself and eat in some cheap little restaurant.'

Léon irritably put down his gold pencil.

'Really, Marthe, you needn't be so cutting! In the first place there aren't any cheap little restaurants . . .'

Marthe's nerves were thoroughly on edge. She gave a sarcastic laugh.

'No one like Léon for summing up a situation in a few well-chosen words! . . . Now, now, Annie, stop looking like a martyr . . . It's this chicken with pears that's driven me frantic . . . Are you two coming? I'm fed up, I'm going home.'

With a peevish gesture, she gathered up her fleecy, trailing skirt and, sweeping the terrace with a contempt-uous gaze, observed:

'Never mind, one day we'll have a little Bayreuth in Paris. And that, my children, would be far more chic . . . and far more sought after!'

This first night has been so appalling, it would be better not even to mention it. Wedged in the middle of the hard mattress, scratched by the coarse cotton sheets, I cau-tiously breathed in the – imaginary . . . ? smell of cabbage that filtered through the windows, under the doors, though the walls. In the end I sprayed an entire bottle of White Carnation over my bed and fell into a sleep filled with absurd voluptuous dreams. It was like looking at slightly caricatured illustrations in a dirty book . . . a debauch in Louis-Philippe costume. Alain in nankeen, and more enterprising than he had ever been; myself in organdie, more revolted than I had ever dreamed . . . But, in any case, those voluminous trousers rendered any consent impossible.

SEVEN

OWING to our having booked our seats almost at the
last moment, I could not sit with Marthe and Léon.
Secretly I was glad to be on my own, away from them.
Standing up, in the dim light of the round lamps that
encircled the auditorium like a broken necklace, I cau-
tiously analysed the odour of burnt rubber and mildewed
cellars. I was not shocked by the grey ugliness of the
sacred fane. Everything, including the low stage and the
black gulf out of which the music would rise, had been
so over-described to me, that it hardly came as anything
new. I waited. Outside, the second fanfare sounded (I
think it was Donner's call). Some foreign women removed their hatpins with a bored, accustomed gesture. I
did the same. Like them, I stared vaguely at the *Fürsten-
loge*, where I could see black shadows moving about and
large bare foreheads tilted forward ... There was no
interest to be found there. I had to wait a little longer,
for the last padded door to be opened for the last time,
showing a patch of blue sky in the aperture, for the last
old lady to have finished coughing once and for all,
before finally the E flat rose from the abyss and growled
like a hidden beast.

'Obviously, it's very fine,' decreed Marthe. 'But it
doesn't have any intervals.'
I was still throbbing, but I concealed my emotion like
a sensual desire. I merely replied that it had not seemed
long to me. But my sister-in-law who was wasting a new
orange dress, the same shade as her hair, thought poorly
of this 'fairy-prologue'.

'My dear, the intervals here are part of the performance. They're something one simply must see . . . ask any of the regular *habitués*. You eat during them, you meet your friends, you exchange impressions at length . . . The spectacle's almost unique. Isn't it, Maugis?'

The great boor imperceptibly raised his shoulders.

' "Unique", that was the word I was looking for. Nevertheless, in here, at least they don't have the cheek to serve that f . . . filthy dish-water tasting of furniture-polish instead of decent beer. To come to Bayreuth to drink that muck makes one wonder how people can be such fatheads!'

He looked as slovenly and dissipated as ever: I searched in vain for some trace of fanatical enthusiasm that might have rehabilitated him in my eyes. For Maugis is one of those who 'discovered' Wagner in France. He has stubbornly imposed him on the French year after year in articles which are an extraordinary mixture of bald scepticism and drunkenly lyrical fervour. I know that Léon despises his flatulent slangy style and that Maugis calls Léon 'a society scribbler' . . . In every other respect, they get on marvellously . . . especially these last two months.

I felt so lost in the theatre's huge restaurant, so far away . . . no, more than that, so *cut off* from everything. I was still inhabited by the demon of the music, the lament of the Rhine maidens was still wailing in my head and conflicting with the deafening clatter of crockery and knives and forks. Frenzied waiters, their black dinner-jackets positively stiff with grease, dashed about, their hands loaded, and the pinkish froth of the beer spilled over into the gravy . . .

'As if we hadn't enough of their beastly *gemischtes-compote*,' grumbled Marthe with extreme resentment. 'That Logi was particularly poor, wasn't he, Maugis?'

'Oh no, not particularly,' he retorted, with an expression of mock indulgence. 'I heard him seventeen years ago in the same part and I thought him undeniably better today.'

Marthe was not listening. She had turned, first her eyes, then her lorgnette, towards the far end of the room.

'But it is . . . it really is her.'

'Is who?'

'Why, the Chessenet! With people I don't know. There, right at the end, at the table against the wall.'

Feeling horribly shaken, as if I had suddenly been dragged back to my old life, I nervously explored the vast chessboard of tables. Yes, that pinkish-flaxen chignon was undoubtedly Valentine Chessenet's.

'Lord, what a bore!' I sighed dejectedly.

Marthe lowered her lorgnette to scrutinize my face.

'Why should it worry you? You can hardly be afraid – here – of her nabbing your Alain again!'

I gave a slight start.

'Again? I wasn't aware . . .'

Maugis, obviously meaning well, broke in with an idiotic, irrelevant remark that silenced Marthe. She tightened her lips, but she watched me out of the corner of her eye. My fork was trembling a little in my hand. Léon gnawed his gold pencil and looked about him with a reporter's eye. Quite suddenly I had a violent desire to take that mollusc by the scruff of his neck and bang his pretty, lifeless face against the table . . . Then my rush of hot blood subsided and I was left amazed at my absurd burst of feeling . . . I think music must have a bad effect on me. The sight of that Chessenet woman had brought Alain back to me and, for one brief instantaneous flash, I saw him lying asleep, unconscious and white as a corpse.

My husband's mistress! Suppose she had been my husband's mistress! ... For two hours, I have been saying this over and over to myself without its conveying any clear picture ... I cannot evoke any image of Madame Chessenet except in full evening dress or in an elegant afternoon outfit, wearing one of those absurdly small hats with which she tries to create a style peculiarly her own ... the Chessenet style! Yet if she had been his mistress, she must have taken off that tight dress, delicately removed that absurd little hat ... But my weary head cannot imagine further than that ... Besides, neither can I see Alain ardently wooing a woman. He never wooed me. He was never imploring, pressing, anxious, jealous ... All he ever gave me was ... a cage. I was contented with that for so long ...

His mistress! Why doesn't that idea make me feel more heartbroken resentment against my husband? Don't I love him at all any more?

I can't think any longer, I'm exhausted. Let's put it all aside. Think, instead, Annie that now you're alone and free ... that you've still many more weeks of freedom ... Free! it's a strange word ... There are birds who think they are free because they are hopping about outside their cage. Only – their wings are clipped.

'Good gracious, aren't you even up yet?'

This morning, all ready dressed to go out, I went into Marthe's room to ask her to come and explore Bayreuth a little with me. I found her still in bed, her red hair loose and dishevelled about her dimpled white shoulders. As I entered, she gave a leap like a carp and turned her plump behind over under the sheets. She yawned and stretched – she goes to bed with her rings on – then she threw me a rapid grey glance from under frowning eyebrows:

'You've already got your outdoor things on! Where are you off to?'

'Nowhere special. I'm just going for a walk. Are you feeling ill?'

'Bad night, headache, feeling lazy...'

'What a pity! Now I'll have to go all alone.'

I went out, after shaking hands with poor old Léon who did not get up from his mahogany table – every bit as ugly as mine – where he was despatching his sixty lines before luncheon.

I felt diffident, all alone in the street. I would not have the courage to buy anything – I spoke German too badly – I would simply look round. The next minute I was gazing into a 'modern-style' shop that was a world in itself – a Wagnerian world. There was a photograph of the Rhine Maidens with their arms twined round each other's shoulders; three hideous stout women, one of whom squinted, wearing flowered headdresses like the one my Luxemburger cook wears on her day out ... Round the poker-work frame writhed seaweed – or earthworms. Price complete with frame? Ten marks. I paid it.

Why so many portraits of Siegfried Wagner? And why only him? Yet other children of 'Cosima's late' as Maugis calls him are certainly no uglier than this young man with a caricature of a nose. The fact that Siegfried conducts the orchestra – and incidentally conducts it rather badly – hardly seems a sufficient excuse ... Everywhere, there was that persistent smell of cabbage ... None of these streets had any character, and, at the end of the Opernstrasse, I hesitated whether to turn right or left.

'The poor lost child, abandoned by its mother,
Even finds refuge in the holy place,'

said a cheeky, birdlike voice behind me.

'Claudine! ... Yes, I don't know which way to go. I'm so unused to going out by myself.'

'Unlike me. At twelve, I used to scamper about like a little rabbit ... incidentally *I* had a white behind too.'

The ... posterior ... really occupies an excessive place in Claudine's conversation. Nevertheless, I find her entirely delightful.

I reflected, as I walked beside this free creature, that it was odd Alain should have allowed me to visit women of dubious – not even dubious – reputation like that Chessenet female and the Cabbage-Rose, who makes sure beforehand that her lovers are expert, and yet forbidden me to see Claudine, who is charming and who makes no secret of the fact that she adores her husband. Weren't those other women far more dangerous for me to frequent than this one?

'I must say, Claudine, I'm surprised to meet you without either Renaud or Fanchette.'

'Fanchette's asleep and, anyway, the coal-dust dirties her paws. My Renaud's working at his *Diplomatic Review* in which he's abusing Delcassé as a stinker. So I've come out so as not to disturb him. And moreover, I've got maggots in my brain this morning.'

'You've got ...?'

'Yes, maggots. But what about you, Annie? What does this mean, you independent little thing, running about alone in a foreign city, without your governess! And where's your leather satchel? And your drawing-book?'

She stood there teasing me, a quaint figure in her abbreviated skirt, her coarse straw boater tilted over her nose, her curly short hair and her triangular face quite brown above the white silk blouse. Her beautiful almost yellow eyes seemed to light up her whole person, like fires blazing in an open field.

'Marthe's resting,' I replied at last. 'She's tired.'

'Tired of what? Of being pawed by Maugis? Oh! Whatever have I said?' she corrected herself, hypocritically putting her hand over her mouth as if to crush back the impudent words . . .

'You think? . . . You think she does . . . that he does what you just said?'

I could not keep the tremor out of my voice. Fool that I was! I knew Claudine would tell me nothing now. She shrugged her shoulders and spun round on one foot.

'Oh, if you listen to everything *I* say! . . . Marthe is like heaps of women I know . . . it amuses her to be raped a little in front of everybody. Alone with a man, it's a different story, somehow, it doesn't make them any less respectable.' I walked pensively beside Claudine. We met Englishwomen – still more of them! – and Americans in silk and lace at ten o'clock in the morning. My companion received a great many glances. She became conscious of this and returned stare for stare with cool self-possession. Only once did she turn round excitedly and pull me by the sleeve.

'What a pretty woman! Did you see her? That blonde with eyes like black coffee?'

'No, I didn't notice.'

'Little fathead! Where are we going?'

'I wasn't going anywhere. I wanted to see a little of the town.'

'The town? Not worth the trouble. It's nothing but postcards and all the rest is hotels. Come along, I know a pretty garden; we can sit down on the grass.'

I had no strength to resist her turbulent will: I adapted

my steps to her long, quick stride. We walked down an ugly street, and then, some way beyond the Schwarzes Ross, we found ourselves in a great empty square, one of those pleasant, melancholy squares, full of lime-trees and statues, so typical of provincial towns.

'What is this square, Claudine?'

'This? I've no idea. Margravine's Square. When in doubt here, I christen everything Margravine's. Come along, Annie, we're nearly there.'

A little gate in the corner of the big square led us into a trim flower-garden that soon expanded into a park, a slightly neglected park that might have belonged to some cool, sleepy château in provincial France.

'This park is . . . what?'

'The Margravine's Park!' asserted Claudine confidently. 'And here we have one of the Margravine's benches, one of the Margravine's soldiers, one of the Margravine's Nannies . . . Green, isn't it? It's restful. You could almost imagine you were in Montigny . . . except it's not nearly, nearly so good.'

We sat down side by side on the soft, crumbling stone of an old bench.

'You live in Montigny, don't you? Is it beautiful country?'

'Beautiful country? I'm as happy there as a plant in a hedge, as a lizard on its wall, as . . . I don't know. There are days when I don't come home from morning to night – when *we* don't come home,' she corrected herself. 'I've taught Renaud to realize how beautiful that country is. When I go there now, he comes too.'

Once again, her intense love for her husband brought on that depression that almost makes me want to cry.

'He follows you everywhere . . . in everything . . . wherever you go, whatever you do.'

'But I follow him too,' said Claudine, surprised. 'That's how we go on ... We follow each other ... without being like each other.'

I bent my head and scratched the sand with the tip of my umbrella.

'How you love each other!'

'Yes,' she answered simply. 'It's like a disease.' She stared into space for a moment, then turned her eyes back to me.

'And you?' she asked abruptly.

I started.

'Me? ... What about me?'

'You don't love your husband?'

'Alain? Why yes, naturally ...'

I drew back, uneasy. Claudine moved closer and burst out impetuously:

'Ah! "Naturally." Right, if you love him naturally, I know what that means. What's more ...'

I wanted to stop her, but it would have been easier to stop a run-away pony!

'What's more, I've often seen you together. He looks like a stick and you look like a wet handkerchief. He's a clumsy idiot, a booby, a brute ...'

I flinched at her gesture as if she had raised her fist at me ...

'Yes, a brute! That carrot-headed fool has been given a wife, but not the faintest glimmering of how to treat her ... Why, it would be glaringly obvious to a seven-months-old baby! "Annie, you can't do this ... Annie, you can't do that ... it simply isn't *done*!" The third time he said that to *me*, I should have answered: "And suppose I make you a cuckold ... would that be considered correct?"'

She brought it out with such comical fury that I burst into simultaneous laughter and tears. The extraordinary creature! She was so heated that she had actually pulled off her hat and was tossing her short hair as if to cool herself.

I did not know how to control myself. I still wanted to cry but most of all I wanted to laugh. Claudine turned to me with a severe face that made her look like her cat.

'There's nothing to laugh about! Nothing to cry about either! You're a softy, a pretty little scrap of chiffon, a crumpled bit of silk and you've no excuse because you don't love your husband.'

'I don't love my . . .'

'No, you don't love anyone!'

Her expression changed. She became more serious:

'For you haven't got a love. Love . . . even a forbidden love . . . would have made you blossom, you supple, barren branch . . . Your husband! Why, if you'd loved him in the real sense of the word, loved as I love!' she said, clasping her delicate hands over her breast in a strangely proud, firm gesture, 'you'd have followed him over land and sea, whether he kissed you or beat you, you'd have followed him like his shadow and like his soul! . . . When one loves in a certain way,' she went on in a lower voice, 'even betrayals become unimportant . . .'

I listened, straining towards her, straining to catch what she was uttering like a prophetess revealing strange truths. I listened with a passionate sense of desolation, never taking my eyes off hers that were staring into the distance. Then she calmed herself and smiled at me as if she had only just noticed my presence.

'Annie, in our fields at home, there's a fragile grass that looks like you . . . a grass with a slender stalk and a heavy head of seed-pods that weighs it down. It has a pretty name that I give you whenever I think of you –

"Drooping Melic". It shivers in the wind, as if it were frightened . . . and it only stands up straight when all its seed-pods are empty . . .'

She threw an affectionate arm round my neck.

'Drooping Melic, how charming you are, more's the pity! I haven't seen a woman since . . . for a long time . . . who was so appealing. Look at me, chicory flowers, eyes fringed like a pool among black rushes, Annie who smells like a rose . . .'

Utterly broken with misery, utterly melted with tenderness, I laid my head on her shoulder and raised my still-wet lashes towards her. She bent down her face and dazzled me with her eyes, bright as a wild animal's and suddenly so dominating that I closed my own, overwhelmed . . .

But the affectionate arm was suddenly withdrawn, leaving me tottering . . . Claudine had leapt to her feet. She had stretched herself taut as a bow and was harshly rubbing her temples.

'Too bad!' she muttered. 'Another minute and . . . After I'd absolutely promised Renaud . . .'

'Promised what?' I asked, still at sea.

Claudine laughed in my face, with an odd expression, displaying her short teeth.

'To . . . to . . . be back at eleven, my child. I've cut it a bit fine . . . Buck up, we might just make it if we hurry . . .'

EIGHT

THE first act of *Parsifal* had just finished and sent us out into the disenchantment of broad daylight. During the three days that followed *Rheingold*, these long intervals which were Marthe's and Léon's delight, have always interrupted my illusion or my intoxication in the most inopportune way. To have to leave Brünhilde, abandoned and menacing, to return to my beflounced sister-in-law, to Léon's finical niggling, to Maugis' inextinguishable thirst, to Valentine Chessenet's washed-out fairness was intolerable. Not to mention the *Achs* and the *Kolossals* and the *Sublimes* and the whole stream of polyglot exclamations poured out by these undiscriminating fanatics! No, no, *no*.

'I'd like to have a theatre entirely to myself,' I declared to Maugis.

'In which you resemble Ludwig of Bavaria,' he replied, taking his lips for a moment from the straw of his hot grog. 'Look where *his* morbid fancy led him. He died after building residences in a style which is only esteemed by the most provincial of pastry-cooks. Meditate on the sad result of solitary self-indulgence.'

I started violently. Leaving that drunkard sitting there and refusing the enormous glass of lemonade Claudine was holding out to me, I went and stood with my back against a pillar, facing the declining sun. Swift clouds were hurrying towards the east and their shadow was all at once chill. Over Bayreuth, the black smoke from the factory chimneys swayed over heavily till a stronger wind swallowed it up in one breath.

A group of Frenchwomen, in straight corsets that

flattened their hips and exaggeratedly long skirts that fitted closely in front and swept out in folds behind them, were talking in high, shrill voices. Their conversation was extremely uninhibited and had nothing to do with the magnificent music. They were talking with that cold animation that is attractive for a minute but becomes exasperating after a quarter of an hour. They were pretty creatures and, even without hearing what they were saying, one could have guessed they belonged to a frail, nervous race, contemptuous and lacking will-power – a race very different, for example, from that calm, red-haired Englishwoman whom they were taking to pieces from top to toe. The latter completely ignored them from where she sat on one of the steps of the porch, displaying her large, ill-shod feet with chaste tranquillity ... Then it was my turn to be stared at and whispered about.

The one who seemed to know everything declared: 'I think she's a young widow who comes every year to the festival on account of one of the tenors ...' I smiled at this ingenious calumny and moved away towards Marthe. Marthe was in her element. Wearing white and mauve and leaning on a tall parasol, she was parading about in her most gracious Marie-Antoinette manner, acknowledging friends from Paris, distributing greetings, making inventories of hats ... But there was that odious Maugis, brushing her skirts as usual! I preferred to retrace my steps and go back to Claudine.

But Claudine was deep in conversation – clasping a huge cream-stuffed cake in her ungloved hand – with a most strange little creature ... That brown Egyptian face, in which the mouth and eyes seemed to be drawn with two parallel strokes of the brush, framed in dancing ringlets like those of a little girl of 1828 ... could it belong to anyone but Mademoiselle Polaire? All the same,

Polaire in Bayreuth seemed so wildly improbable that I could hardly believe my eyes!

Both were supple and slender, both intensely lively, each wore a little bow on her forehead at the edge of her parting – Polaire's white, Claudine's black. The people who were avidly staring at them declared they looked like twins. I did not agree. Claudine's hair was more boyish and rebellious and her eyes did not evoke the east as Polaire's did. Those admirable Egyptian eyes of Polaire's have more gloom, more defiance – and more subservience – in their expression. All the same, there was a resemblance. Passing behind them, Renaud gave their two short manes a quick, affectionate tweak; then, laughing at my stupefied face, he said:

'Yes, Annie, it positively is Polaire, our little lily.'

'Their Tiger-Lily,' added Maugis, who was mimicking a cake-walk with extravagant nigger-minstrel's hip wrigglings. I was ashamed to find myself laughing at his contortions as he sang with a nasal twang:

> *'She draws niggers like a crowd of flies*
> *She is my sweetest one, my baby Tiger-Lily!'*

So now I had all the information I needed!

Insensibly, I had drawn closer to the two friends in my curiosity ... Claudine caught sight of me and beckoned me with an imperious gesture. Feeling very self-conscious, I found myself confronting this little actress who barely glanced at me, being far too busy standing on one foot, tossing back her dark hair that had tawny glints in it, and feverishly explaining something or other in a throaty, twanging voice.

'You see, Claudine, if I mean to do serious drama, I've got to know all the serious drama before my time. So I've come to Bayroot to get educated.'

'It was your duty,' said Claudine with grave approval

– though her tobacco-brown eyes were dancing with jubilant mischief.

'They've put me up right at the other end of the town, at the back of beyond – over there, at the Bamboo Cabin . . .'

Claudine saw my astonishment at the peculiar name of the hotel and informed me, with angelic kindness:

'It's the Margravine's bamboo.'

'It doesn't matter,' went on Polaire. 'I don't regret coming all this way, although! . . . You know, at Madame Marchand's, they produced it quite differently from here, and besides, their Wagner isn't anything to make you fall flat on your fanny! . . . As to his music, why it's just like a band! Makes me want to salute and slap my right thigh.'

'Just the way Annie expresses it,' slipped in Claudine, with a glance at me.

'Ah, Madame says that too? Pleased to meet you . . . What was I saying? Oh, yes . . . That makes it twice I've been to *Parsifal* to make sure, wherever you go, you find lousy people. You saw Kundry, that bandeau she had round her forehead, and then those flowers, and that veil hanging down? Well, that's exactly the head-dress Landorff designed for me for the Winter-garten in Berlin, that year I bored myself stiff singing *Little Cohn*!'

Polaire exulted for a moment, then paused for breath, oscillating on her high heels and wriggling her abnormally small waist which she could have belted with a man's collar.

'You ought to sue,' Claudine advised fervently.

Polaire started like a fawn and launched forth again:

'Never, it's beneath me . . .' (her beautiful eyes darkened). '*I'm* not like other women. Anyway, what's the good? Sue these Boches? Oh, bother . . . where's my nail buffer got to? . . . Besides there'd be no end to it . . .

Actually again in their *Parsifal* ... just listen ... in act three when the fat man's dipping in the water and that hairy bloke's sprinkling him, well that chap's attitude, with his hands folded flat and his body turned at that three-quarter angle is *absolutely* my gesture in *Berber Song*, that he's pinched from me. Just imagine my agony! And all my side, Claudine, the right of my corsets, all the bones are broken!'

I studied her fascinating face, so mobile that it was like watching a cinema film as it swiftly registered in turn excitement, rebellion, a Negro ferocity, an enigmatic melancholy whose shadow was dispersed by an abrupt, jerky laugh as Polaire flung up her pointed chin like a dog baying the moon. Then all at once, she simply left us standing, with a grave childish good-bye, like a well-brought-up little girl's.

For a moment, I followed her with my eyes, watching her swift walk, the deft way she threaded her way through the groups, with a quick swing of her hips and broken gestures that reminded one of her broken syntax, her whole body leaning slightly forward, like a clever animal walking on its hind legs.

'A sixteen-inch waist!' said Claudine reflectively.

'It's a size in shoes, not in belts.'

'Annie? ... Annie, I'm talking to you!'

'Yes, yes, I'm listening!' I said, coming to with a start.

'What have I just been talking about?'

Under my sister-in-law's inquisitorial eye, I became confused and averted my head.

'I don't know, Marthe.'

She shrugged her shoulders which one could almost see showing pink under a white lace bodice with deep-cut armholes. A wildly indecent bodice ... but since it is high-necked, Marthe displays herself like that in the street and remains perfectly cool and collected under the gaze of the men. I am the one who is embarrassed.

Armed with a spray, she was over-lavishly scenting her pinkish-red hair – her beautiful hair that is as vital and rebellious as she is.

'That's enough, Marthe, that's enough, you smell too good as it is.'

'Never too good. For one thing, I'm always afraid of people saying I smell like a red-head! Now that you've come down from your cloud, I'll start all over again. We're dining tonight at the Berlin ... Maugis is standing treats.'

'Again!'

The word had slipped out in spite of me and Marthe spiked it in mid-air with a glance as sharp as a dagger.

'What d'you mean – "again"? Anyone would think we were sponging on Maugis. It's his turn, we invited him the day before yesterday.'

'And last night?'

'Last night? That was entirely different – he wanted to show us that Sammet place – it's supposed to be a historic eating house. Anyway, the food was revolting in that hole – tough meat and flabby fish. He definitely owes us a decent meal to make up for it.'

'Owes you and Léon, maybe, but not me.'

'It shows his good manners, always including you too.'

'Good manners ... how much I wish that just for tonight he'd revert to his normal ones!'

Marthe combed her black hair with savage little tugs.

'Charming! Quite a neat sarcasm! You're definitely coming on. Is it seeing so much of Claudine?'

She put so much acidity into the question that I shivered as if she had scratched me with the tip of her nails.

'I've less to lose by seeing so much of Claudine than you have by seeing so much of Maugis.'

She turned on me; her piled-up hair was like a helmet of writhing flames.

'Advice? You've got a ruddy cheek! Yes, a ruddy cheek to meddle in my affairs and take it on yourself to tell me how to behave. I've got a husband to do that, you know! And I'm amazed you dare to find anything improper in something Léon accepts as perfectly all right!'

'*Please*, Marthe . . .'

'Had enough, eh? Well, mind you don't let it happen again! Monsieur Maugis is simply a very devoted friend.'

'Marthe, I implore you not to go on. Insult me as much as you like but don't try and set up "Monsieur Maugis" as a perfectly blameless, devoted friend and Léon as a despotic husband . . . You can't think me quite such a fool!'

She had not expected this. She held her breath, with an effort, for she was panting with fury. She struggled hard with herself for a long minute, and finally mastered herself with a power that proved to me how frequent these rages were.

'Now, now Annie . . . don't take advantage of me. You know how easily I flare up. I believe you're teasing me on purpose . . .'

She smiled, the corners of her mouth still quivering.

'You're coming to dinner with us, aren't you?'

I still hesitated. She put her arm round my waist, clever and coaxing as when she wanted to smooth down Alain.

'You owe that to my reputation! Just think if people see all four of us together, they may think it's you that Maugis is running after!'

117

We were all good friends again, but I could feel our friendship cracking like a white frost in the sun. I was very tired. Ever since yesterday a migraine had been dully threatening me; this little scene had brought it on in full force. Nevertheless, I felt it was almost worth it. Only a month ago, I would not have had the courage to tell Marthe even half of what I was thinking . . .

As we drove to the *Flying Dutchman*, I sat perfectly mute in the carriage, with my finger pressed to my temple, too stupefied to utter a word. Léon asked compassionately:

'Migraine, Annie?'

'Yes, unfortunately.'

He nodded his head and gazed at me sympathetically with his gentle, spaniel-like eyes. For some time, I too have felt extremely sorry for him. If Marthe wears the trousers, *he* may well be wearing . . . Claudine would have brought out the word without the slightest hesitation. My sister-in-law, sitting tranquilly beside me, was flouring her cheeks in an effort to overcome the heat.

'We shan't see Maugis up there,' observed my brother-in-law, 'he's keeping to his room.'

'Ah!' ejaculated Marthe indifferently.

Her lips had tightened as if to suppress a smile.

'Is he ill?' I asked. 'Perhaps slightly too many grogs last night?'

'No. But he says the *Flying Dutchman* is a piece of sentamental filth, the dregs of Italian-German opera and all the performers lousy. I assure you, Annie, those were his exact words. He also added that the mere thought of Daland the fisherman, Senta's father, gives him a violent pain in his guts.'

'It's a somewhat personal type of criticism,' I said ungraciously.

Marthe looked away and did not seem anxious to pursue the conversation. On our left, the empty carriages were returning at a faster trot, raising clouds of dust, whereas we were climbing the hill almost at a walk, jammed in the file of traffic ... I have only seen it four times, that brick theatre (Claudine is perfectly right, it *does* look like a gasometer), the brightly-dressed crowd surrounding it, the row of local inhabitants stupidly sneering at the visitors, yet every time I look at that scene again, I feel the same almost physical impatience that used to come over me sometimes in Paris when I stared at the restricted, intolerably well-known view from my bedroom window. But in those days I had less sensitive nerves and a master who made it his business to keep me dull-witted. I was almost afraid to think and to look about me.

I would not admit to anyone but myself and to these useless pages of my diary, how disillusioned I am with Bayreuth. There is nothing much to choose between an interval during *Parsifal* and a Paris tea-party – a 'five o'clock' at my sister-in-law Marthe's or at that loathsome Valentine Chessenet's. The same ill-natured tittle-tattle; the same passion for gossip and scandal, even for out-and-out slander; the same trivial small talk in which the latest fashions, the latest composers, greed, and indecency are all equally entertaining topics.

Once again I longed to get away. At Arriège, I used to gaze at the rift of light between two mountain peaks: here my eyes follow the trails of smoke as they stream away to the east ... Where could I escape from monotonous sameness, from the all too well-known, from mediocrity and malice? Perhaps I ought to have done what Claudine said ... accompanied Alain in spite of himself? No, for with Alain – and in him – I should only have found once again the very things I want to escape from ... Migraine, alas, is a depressing and realistic adviser and I listened to it more attentively than I did to the *Flying Dutchman* ... Ether, oblivion, cool unconsciousness ... those were the only things that attracted me ... A mark in the hand of the old man who showed us into our seats bought me my liberty and authorized my silent escape ... 'This lady is ill ...'

I ran, I jumped into a carriage, and soon I was in my room where Toby, who was sleeping sentimentally on my slippers, barked affectionately to see me back so soon. *He* loves me! And someone else loves me – *I* do! I take more pleasure in looking at myself nowadays. Away from that white man whose gleaming skin made me seem so black, I find myself prettier and exactly, as Marthe said, like a slender fine brownstone jar, with two wild chicory flowers in it. Claudine talked as if she were thinking aloud: 'Blue flowers, look at me – eyes fringed like a pool among black rushes ...' But her friendly arm had withdrawn ...

At last, at last, I was lying half-undressed face down on the bed with the heavenly bottle under my nostrils. Suddenly, I could feel myself flying; I could feel the cool sting of imaginary drops of water all over my body; the cruel blacksmith's arm grew slacker and slacker ... But I was still awake under my semi-drunken stupor; I did not want that heavy sleep, that swoon from which one emerges nauseated. All I wanted from the little Genie of ether, that crafty comforter with the, sweet ambiguous smile, was the fanning of wings and the gentle rocking that turned my bed into a swing ...

The brief, furious barking of the little dog awakened me. Frozen with terror, I groped for my watch. Nonsense, they wouldn't search for me up there, by the 'gasometer' ... They were far too concerned with their own affairs to be concerned about me ... All told, my escape and my brief drunken stupor had taken up only an hour. I thought it had been far longer. 'Oh, be quiet,' I implored Toby, 'for goodness' sake be quiet ... my ears cannot bear noise just now ...'

He obeyed regretfully, laid his square nose on his paws and blew out his long dewlaps, still barking internally. My good little watch-dog, my little black friend, I shall take you wherever I go ... He listened and I listened too; a door shut in the room next to mine – Marthe's room. No doubt it was the ever-obliging Madame Meider who had gone in to 'tidy things' – to open the little silver boxes and straighten out the illustrated Paris papers scrunched up into balls in the waste-paper basket.

Yesterday, as I passed through the hall, I caught the four little Meider girls in pinafores, carefully smoothing out a crumpled number of *La Vie en rose* with their grubby hands. The four little Meider girls will learn French from it – and something else into the bargain.

No, it was not Madame Meider. They were speaking French ... Why, it was Marthe! Marthe who had come to inquire after me: I had not expected such devoted solicitude! Marthe's voice and a man's. Léon? No.

Half-undressed, sitting on my bed with my legs dangling over the edge, I strained my ears to hear but I could not manage to. The ether was still buzzing, faintly, in my ears ...

My chignon was coming down. A tortoiseshell hairpin slid down the nape of my neck, soft and cold as a little snake. Whatever must I have looked like, with my bodice undone and my skirt pulled up showing my dusky skin and my shoes still on my feet! The greenish mirror reflected my ravaged face – pallid lips; glazed eyes, puckered at the outer corners, with purple shadows under them like bruises ... But whoever was that talking in Marthe's bedroom?

There was an incessant murmur of voices, punctuated

now and then by a loud laugh or by an ejaculation from my sister-in-law ... Definitely, a very peculiar kind of conversation ...

Suddenly there was a shriek! A man's voice let out an oath, then Marthe's voice exclaimed irritably: 'Keep your foot still, can't you?'

Shocked to the core, for Marthe had used the familiar *tu* which she never used to her husband, I did up my blouse with trembling hands and pulled down my skirt as if someone had suddenly come into the room. My clumsy fingers kept ineffectively sticking the same pin into my hair a dozen times without making it stay up ... Whoever could it be behind that wall, alone with Marthe?

There was complete silence now. What ought I to do? Suppose the *man* had hurt Marthe? Ah, how I wished he *had* done her some physical injury, that he had been a thief, a prowler armed with a knife, for now I was imagining all sorts of things more revolting than any crime going on behind that door. I wanted to see, I wanted to know ...

I grabbed the handle and pushed the door open with all my might, one hand put up to shield my face as if I were afraid someone was going to hit me.

What I saw, without fully taking it in at first, was Marthe's milky-white back and her plump shoulders naked above her pulled-down chemise. Then I realized, to my horror, she was sitting on Maugis' knees. Maugis, scarlet in the face, was slumped in an armchair ... apparently fully dressed. Marthe screamed, then leapt to her feet revealing the disarray of that loathsome man with her.

Planted there squarely in front of me, in a pair of long linen drawers with voluminous, frilly legs, with her white face and her wobbling red chignon, she irresistibly suggested a female clown at a carnival. But what a tragic clown, paler than the traditional flour could make her, her eyes dilated and deadly! I stood there, unable to speak.

Maugis found his tongue first. He said in a caddishly flippant way:

'Come on, Marthe, now the kid's caught us out, we might as well finish our little orgy ... What's the risk?'

With a curt nod, she showed him the door. Then she bore down on me and pushed me into my room so roughly that I staggered and nearly fell.

'What are you doing here? Did you follow us?'

'Good heavens, no!'

'You're lying!'

I straightened myself up and dared to look her in the face.

'No, I'm not lying. I had a migraine and I came home. I gave something to the man at the door so that he'd let me through. I ...'

Marthe laughed, without opening her mouth, as if she had hiccups.

'Ah, so you know that dodge too ... the mark to the man at the door? You're ripe for the big stuff now, Alain had better watch out ... I admit your migraine, but why the hell did you come bursting into my bedroom?'

How bold a woman can be! This one was back in her element, she was once again the indomitable little flame-thrower on the barricade. With her hands on her hips, she would have braved an army, with the same white face, the same hard, unflinching eyes ...

'Are you going to talk? What do you expect to get for running off to Léon to tell him he's a cuckold?'

I blushed, both at the word and at the suspicion.

'I shan't do that, Marthe. You know that quite well.'

She stared at me for a moment, her eyebrows raised.

'Nobility of soul? No. I can't swallow that. More likely a trick, to keep a hold on me for the rest of my life. You can get rid of that notion. I'd rather go and tell that other imbecile myself.'

I made a gesture of weary impatience.

'You don't understand me. It isn't only the ... the thing itself that shocks me ... it's your choosing that cad ... Oh, Marthe, *that* man of all men ...'

That wounded her, and she bit her lip. Then she shrugged her shoulders, with a gesture at once sad and cynical.

'Yes, yes. You're another of those simpletons for whom adultery ... a conventional word you like, eh? ... ought to be hidden in bowers of flowers, and to be ennobled by passion, by the beauty of the lovers, by their oblivion of the world ... There, there my poor girl, keep your illusions! Personally I'll keep my own particular worries and my own particular tastes ... That cad as you call him, possesses among other qualities an open purse, a kind of lewd wit I rather enjoy, and the tact to ignore jealousy. He smells of the bar? Maybe he does. Even so, I much prefer that smell to Léon's – he smells of cold veal.'

As if suddenly exhausted, she collapsed on a chair.

'Everyone hasn't the luck to sleep with Alain, my dear. In fact it's a privilege reserved to a small number of females ... whom I don't envy all that much.'

What was she going to say next? She flashed me a malicious smile before adding:

'Anyway, without wishing to be unjust to him, that delicious brother of mine must be a rotten lover. "Toc, toc, that's that. See you again soon, dear lady." Eh?'

I turned away my head; there were tears in my eyes. Marthe swiftly hooked up her dress, pinned on her hat and went on talking in a dry, feverish voice:

'... So I can't understand why Valentine Chessenet

was crazy about him for so long ... considering she's an expert in men ...'

It was indeed the name I was dreading. But I too was brave in my own way; I waited for what was to come without flinching.

My sister-in-law put on her gloves, grabbed her parasol and opened the door.

'Eighteen months, my dear, eighteen months of letter-writing and regular meetings. Twice a week ... as regularly as a piano lesson.'

I stroked the little bull-terrier with a hand that had gone quite cold. Marthe lowered the veil of a hat entirely covered with roses, licked the superfluous rouge off her lips and studied me covertly in the glass. But I made sure she saw nothing.

'Was it a long time ago, Marthe? I certainly heard plenty of rumours but nothing very precise.'

'A long time ago? Yes, quite a long time. It's been over since last Christmas ... so I'm told. Nearly eight months – it's ancient history ... Farewell, noble soul!'

She slammed the door. She was undoubtedly telling herself: 'I've hit back. A good, telling blow! Let Annie talk now if she likes! I've had my revenge in advance.'

She did not know that what she thought was a mortal blow had been dealt not at a person but only at her empty garment.

When she had gone, I felt utterly exhausted, physically and mentally. Every muscle in my body was stiff and aching; my mind was a whirling fog in which depression, the shame and shock of what I had seen, the inability to decide what I ought to do, all mingled together in wearying confusion. At last I was clearly conscious of one thing – the impossibility of seeing Marthe every day, every hour, without seeing the odious face of that

gross, almost fully-clothed man beside her insolent grace
... Was that adultery and could one believe that what
they were doing bore any resemblance to love? Alain's
brief, monotonous love-making did not soil me as much
as that, and, thank God, if I had to choose ... But I did
not want to choose.

Neither did I want to stay on here, even though I
would not hear *Tristan*, and not see Claudine again ...
Good-bye, elusive Claudine! For, ever since that troubled
hour when she guessed so much of my misery, when I
felt so close to loving her, Claudine has avoided any
occasion of seeing me alone and smiles at me from a distance as if at some place she were sorry to leave.

No, I must look for some other way out! The summer
was nearly over. For the first time, I realized that Alain
would soon be embarking on his return voyage and I
childishly pictured him loaded with great sacks of gold,
red gold like his hair ...

A paragraph from his last letter came back to my
mind: 'I have noticed, my dear Annie, that certain of
the women in this country resemble you in type. The
most pleasing of them have, like you, long, heavy black
hair, beautiful thick eyelashes, smooth brown skins, and
the same taste for idleness and day-dreaming. But the
climate here explains and excuses these tendencies of
theirs. Perhaps living here might have altered many
things between us ...'

What! Could that clear-cut, positive mind become
hazy too? Was he confusedly thinking of revising and
modifying our ... our 'timetable'? Mercy, how many
more changes, surprises, disillusions! I was weary at the
prospect of having to begin my life all over again. Some
clean, quiet corner; new faces which conveyed nothing
to me of what was going on behind them ... that was all,
absolutely all, I wanted!

With a great effort, I got up and went off to look for my maid ... I found her in the kitchen, surrounded by the four ecstatic little Meiders to whom she was singing in a robust baritone voice:

> '*I lov-er yew with love so trew*
> *Night and day, I dream of yew* ...'

'Léonie, I want you to pack my things. I'm leaving at once.'

She followed me, too dumbfounded to answer. The four little Meiders would never know the end of that waltz...

Cantankerously, she dived into my trunk.

'Am I to pack Madame Léon's trunk too?'

'No, no I'm leaving alone, with you and Toby.' I added nervously: 'I've received a telegram.'

Léonie's back expressed complete disbelief.

'You'll take a cab to the station with the luggage as soon as you're ready. I'll meet you there with the dog.'

I was so terrified they would return! I kept glancing every minute at my watch. For once I blessed those interminable performances. At least they would cover my escape.

I paid my bill without looking at it and left an enormous tip that made the four little girls in pinafores jump for joy. The Franconians have no false pride!

At last, there I was alone with Toby, wearing his leather and badger-hair travelling collar. His little black face following my every movement; he understood and sat patiently waiting, his metal lead trailing on the carpet. I had still a quarter of an hour to spare. I wrote a hurried note to Marthe and sealed it in an envelope. 'I'm leaving for Paris. Make whatever explanation you like to Léon.'

My heart was heavy at the thought of how alone I was

in the world. I would like to have left a more affectionate farewell message to someone ... but to whom? Suddenly, I thought I knew.

My dear Claudine,

Something unexpected forces me to leave immediately. It's a very upsetting, very hurried departure. But don't go and suppose some accident has happened to Alain or Marthe – or to me. I am leaving because everything here oppresses me. Bayreuth is not far enough from Arriège, nor Arriège far enough from Paris, to which I am returning.

You have made me see only too clearly that where there is no great love there is only mediocrity or misery. I do not know yet what remedy I shall find: I am going away to make a change, and to wait.

Perhaps you could have kept me here, you who radiate faith and tenderness. But, ever since the Margravine's garden, you no longer seem to want to. No doubt you are justified. It is right that you should keep that flame that you warmed me with for a moment whole and intact for Renaud.

At least write me a letter – just one letter. Comfort me and tell me, even if you have to lie, that my misery is not beyond all alleviation. For the thought of Alain's return fills me with such troubled apprehension that even hope seems dim and unreal to me.

Good-bye ... give me some advice. Let me lay my head, in spirit, on your shoulder as I did in the Margravine's garden.

Annie

NINE

It was eleven in the morning when I arrived in Paris. It looked arid and dejected as Paris always does at the end of summer. I felt empty and sick: I seemed to have come back from the other end of the world with only one desire, to lie down on the spot and go to sleep. Leaving Léonie to struggle with the Customs, I fled straight home in a cab ...

When it stopped outside the house, the concierge, out of uniform and in shirtsleeves, came out on the doorstep with his wife, my cook. Her mottled cheeks turned streaky white and red at the sight of me ... Absent-mindedly, I read on their dull faces surprise, embarrassment, and the offended dignity of correct servants confronted with someone who has behaved incorrectly ...

'It's Madame! ... But we never received Madame's telegram!'

'That's because I didn't send one.'

'Ah, that's what I said too ... Monsieur is not with Madame?'

'Obviously not. Get me some lunch as soon as possible ... Anything will do ... some eggs, a cutlet ... Léonie's following on with the luggage.'

I walked slowly up the stairs, followed by the concierge who hastily put on a green livery coat with tarnished buttons. I stared, feeling like a stranger, at this little house Alain had insisted on buying ... Personally, I had not wanted it in the least. But my opinion had not been asked ... Nevertheless, I think that, below a certain price, a small town house is more commonplace and more uncomfortable than a flat ...

What did all that matter now? I felt as indifferent as if I were a traveller arriving at a hotel. There were dirty finger-marks on the white door of my bedroom ... the electric light bulb in the passage had gone ... From force of habit I opened my mouth to order the paint to be washed, and the bulb renewed ... Then I changed my mind and turned away.

When I opened the door of my yellow and white bedroom, I softened a trifle and lost some of my courage. On that little lacquered desk, where not much dust was visible, I had written the first lines of my notebook ... In that great flat bed where my light weight barely makes a hollow, I had experienced, as if in a dream, migraine, fear, resignation, the fleeting shadow of love, unsatisfied desire. What should I dream about in it now, deprived of my fear, my resignation, of even the shadow of love? It was extraordinary that a creature as weak as myself, so dependent on physical and moral support, should somehow find herself alone and not perish at once like a convolvulus whose tendrils have been torn away from what they clung to. Perhaps one did wither away like that – so quickly ... Mechanically, I went over and looked at myself in the glass over the chimney-piece.

I would not have been astonished to see a wasted, diminished Annie appear in the glass, an Annie with even narrower shoulders and an even more drooping body than before the summer began ... My reflection surprised me and I leant on my elbows to study it at closer range.

The dark hair, matted by the night in the train, made a harsh frame to the still slender oval of a brown face. But that pucker of weariness at the corners of the lips was not the only thing that altered the line of the mouth, a mouth firmer and less beseeching than formerly ... As to the eyes, their gaze was more direct; the eyelids kept steady instead of constantly fluttering and drooping under the weight of the silky lashes. I would never be able to look at you again, 'wild chicory flowers', my amazingly clear eyes, my one real beauty, without thinking of Claudine bending down over them and saying teasingly: 'Annie, they're so clear, you can see right through to the other side.' Alas, it was true. Clear as an empty bottle. Moved by that memory, vaguely intoxicated by the novelty of my reflected image, I bent my head and touched my ungloved hand with my lips ...

'Am I to unpack Madame's trunk?'

Léonie had come in, out of breath, and was running a hostile eye over the room which would have to be given 'a thorough good do'.

'I don't know, Léonie ... I'm waiting for a letter ... Only take out the silk dresses and petticoats – the rest can wait ...'

'Very good, Madame. Actually I've got a letter for you here from Monsieur that the porter was going to send on to Germany.'

I snatched the unexpected letter from her. So as to read it by myself, I went off into Alain's study where I pushed back the shutters myself.

My dear Annie,

It is a very tired husband who is writing to you. Don't be alarmed; I said 'tired', not 'ill'. I have had a hard struggle. I have already told you of the difficulties of converting bulls into ready money and I will tell you again in more detail when I see you. I am delighted to have emerged from them honourably and to be bringing back a handsome sum. You should be grateful to me, Annie, for undertaking this journey which enables me to increase the amenities of our home and to offer you a sable

*stole as handsome as the one belonging to Madame ...
you know whom I mean? ... my sister disrespectfully
calls her:'the Chessenet'.*

*The sun is oppressive at this hour so I am taking advantage of it to catch up with my correspondence. Out in the
courtyard a girl is sitting sewing, or pretending to sew.
There is really a quite singular resemblance. which I have
remarked many times, between her bent, motionless profile, with the chignon on the nape of the neck, and yours,
Annie. The red flower is an addition, of course, so is the
little yellow shawl. All the same, it amuses me to watch
her and makes my thoughts stray towards you and towards my return which is now only a matter of
days ...*

Of days! It was true, he had been gone a long time ...
But *days!* I had begun to believe he would never return.
And now he was going to come back, he was going to
leave that distant land, that dark girl who looked like me
and whom perhaps, on stormy nights, he called Annie ...
He was going to come back and I had not yet decided my
fate and plucked up courage against myself and against
him!

Without picking up the letter I had dropped on the
carpet, I gazed about me reflectively. This study, which
serves as a smoking-room had not kept any imprint of its
master. There was nothing lying about in it and nothing
in it to charm. The tapestry that had been taken down
for the summer left a great panel of white, unpapered
wall. I felt thoroughly miserable here; I would not stay
on in Paris.

'Léonie!'

The good policeman came running, a skirt dangling
from each of her forefingers.

'Léonie, I want to leave tomorrow for Casamène.'

'For Casamène. Oh, goodness me, no!'

'What do you mean, no?'

'Madame hasn't written to the gardener's wife, the house is shut up and hasn't been cleaned, there won't be any food got in. And besides I need a good two days for the things that needs doing here – there's Madame's everyday skirts that's got their linings torn, there's the white linen dress what we couldn't find a cleaner for in Germany and the petticoat what goes with it as needs new lace putting on, and then there's . . .'

I put both hands over my ears – Léonie's grammar showed she was seriously upset.

'That'll do, that'll do! You shall have two days for all that. Only write yourself to the gardener's wife and tell her . . .' (I hesitated for a moment) '. . . tell her I'm only bringing you. She's to do the cooking.'

'Very good, Madame.'

Léonie made a dignified exit. Once again, I had offended her. One has to be careful with one's subordinates! All the servants who have passed through this house have been hypersensitives, ill-tempered ones too, who fiercely resented other people's changes of mood and let it appear on their faces – when Alain was absent.

I am leaving tomorrow. It is high time, my patience is worn out. All this setting of my married life has become intolerable to me, even the Louis XV drawing-room where on Fridays I used to wait, meek and terrified, for the ring that announced the first caller. I exaggerate: in those days which seem strangely far away I was more meek than terrified and almost happy in a timid, colourless way. Is my lot any better today, wandering hither and thither, demoralized yet more self-willed? It's a very arduous problem for such a tired brain.

I am leaving nothing of myself behind in this little house, tall and narrow as a tower. Alain did not want

Grandmother Lajarrisse's furniture; it has remained at Casamène. Some books, two or three photographs of Annie – the rest belongs to my husband.

Three years ago I gave him a little English desk which he has graciously kept ever since in his study. Today I indiscreetly pulled the brass handle of the drawer, which resisted. A methodical man locks his drawers when he goes off on a long journey. Looking at it closer, I discovered it was sealed with a little, almost invisible strip of gummed paper ... Obviously my husband did not completely trust his domestic staff. But had he only been thinking of his man-servant when he devised such a carefully concealed precaution ? ... Suddenly, I had a vision of Marthe's venomous face: 'Eighteen months of continuous correspondence and regular meetings ...'

I felt I would rather like to know what Valentine Chessenet's style was like. I can swear that it was not a sudden access of physical jealousy or some feverish compulsion that made me want to open that drawer ... It was simply that I reached a stage where scruples seemed an absurd luxury ...

One after another, all the keys on my little bunch proved useless for the English lock. I disliked the idea of asking anyone's assistance. I looked round and saw a flat metal ruler lying on the writing table ... Yes, it would do to make a lever under the drawer. What hard work it was ! The exertion made me hot and I broke my thumb-nail, such a well-manicured little pink nail on my brown hand. There was an appallingly loud crack ... suppose the servants came in, thinking there had been an accident ? I listened for a moment, terrified. Thieves must often die of heart-failure !

The light ash-wood had split. A little more work and

the whole front of the pretty desk was smashed and ripped off. It fell to the ground, followed by an avalanche of papers.

I felt as abashed as a little girl who had upset a box of chocolates. Where should I begin? It would not take long; each little bundle, methodically secured by a rubber band, bore a label.

Here were *Receipted Bills*, here were *Title Deeds*, here were *Papers concerning lawsuit over building-plots* (what building-plots?), then came *Receipts from Marthe* (ah?), *Letters from Annie* (three in all), *Letters from Andrée* (but which Andrée?), letters ... letters ... letters ... ah, at last! *Letters from Valent*:

I went over to the door and quietly locked it. Then, sitting on the floor, I spread the quite thick bundle out on my lap.

'My beloved Carrots ...' 'My little white man.' (She too!) 'Dear Friend.' 'Monsieur.' 'Naughty boy.' 'Fickle brute.' 'My copper coffee-pot ...' The appellations certainly varied considerably more than the theme of the letters. Nevertheless, it had been a complete idyll. One could follow it chronologically from the first little note: 'I made a fatal error by giving myself so quickly ...' up to 'There is nothing I shall not do to get you back. I shall even seek you out at home with your little black goose ...'

In the margin on the back of these letters, Alain had noted in his stiff writing: 'Received the ...' 'Answered the ... by telegram.' I would have recognized him just by that trait. Ah! *She* could call him beloved Carrots, white pussy-cat, tea-pot, coffee-pot, whatever she fancied ... he would still be the same man!

What should I do with all this stuff? Send the packet of letters to Alain's address, in a sealed envelope addressed in my writing? That was what people did in novels. But he would think I still loved him and was jealous. No ... I left all the papers on the floor at the foot of the ravaged desk, along with the flat ruler and my bunch of little keys. The only thing I took away was *Letters from Annie*. My pillaging had made glorious havoc of that tidy soulless room ... I would give a good deal to see Alain's face when he returns!

A blue envelope lay beside my cup on the breakfast tray. I guessed more by the fat round handwriting than by the Bavarian stamp that it was Claudine's reply. She had taken pity on me and answered quickly ... Her handwriting was like her; sensual, lively, and upright. The loops were short and graceful; the crosses of the T's exaggerated and masterful.

My sweet Annie,

So it will be a long time before I see them again, those unique eyes that you hide so often behind your lashes, like a garden behind a grille, for I imagine you have gone off on a long journey ... And whatever gave you the idea of asking me for an itinerary? I am neither Cook's nor Paul Bourget. Anyway, we'll see about that in a moment. First I must tell you the most urgent thing, which is as banal as a sensational news item.

On the day after your departure, I did not see the Léon ménage at Tristan. Your brother-in-law's absence was nothing – but Marthe missing the intervals of Tristan, the most sensational ones after Parsifal! We returned from the theatre on foot as usual, me hanging on the arm of my dear great man, and we thought we'd both go a little out of our way to inquire after Marthe. Horrors! The respectable Melder home was open to all comers and four little girls in pink pinafores were scurrying about like rats. Finally, I caught sight of Marthe with her red mane standing on end, who slammed the door in our face to prevent us from entering ... Renaud parleyed with a maid, listened to what she was moaning in Bavarian punctuated by cries of Yo! and led me away, so astonished that he almost looked stupid ... I exaggerate.

Do you know what, Annie? Léon had just poisoned himself like a shop girl whose young man has chucked her! He had drunk laudanum and so enthusiastically that he had given himself appalling indigestion! You'll immediately think that Liane's suicide must have haunted that eminently Parisian brain. Not at all. In the course of a lively scene, Marthe, in a very irritable mood – history does not record why – had called her spouse 'cuckold' so frequently and with so much conviction that the wretched man no longer doubted what is called in journalese 'the extent of his misfortune'.

The next day I went out to reconnoitre on my own. Marthe received me like a model wife, told me about the 'fatal mistake' and got up a dozen times to rush to the invalid's bedside ... Maugis was not there because an urgent telegram had summoned him to Béziers the night before. It's curious, all the same, Annie, how many urgent departures one sees among the French colony at Bayreuth!

Don't be alarmed, nervous child; the suicide is going on well. Marthe nurses him like a horse who's due to run in the Grand-Prix. In a few days he'll be fit enough to get back to his work at the rate of eighty lines a day instead of sixty to make up for lost time. Your sister-in-law is an intelligent woman who understands to perfection that the situation of a married woman is far superior to that of a divorced one, or to certain widowhoods, even of a lucrative kind.

Now you are up to date with the news. Let us talk about you. About you, you embarrassing little creature, so slow at getting to know herself; so swift, when the appointed day came to fly away, silent, and black-capped, like a migrating swallow.

You are going away, and your flight and your letter are like a reproach to me. How much I regret you, Annie, who smells like a rose! You mustn't be angry with me for that. I am only a poor brute who loves beauty and weakness and trust, and when a little spirit like yours leans on mine, when a mouth yearns, like yours, towards mine, I find it very hard to understand why I must not embellish both the one and the other with a kiss. I tell you I still don't properly understand the reason, although it has been explained to me.

People must have spoken to you, Annie, about me and a woman friend whom I loved too simply, too completely. She was a vicious, fascinating seducer, that Rézi; she tried to put her naked blonde loveliness between me and Renaud and give herself the literary pleasure of betraying us both ... Because of her, I have promised Renaud – and Claudine too – to forget there may be weak, tempting, pretty creatures whom a gesture of mine might charm and enslave ...

You are going away and I can guess that you are all confused in your mind. I hope, for your sake and his, that your husband will not be coming back at once. You are neither sufficiently clear-sighted nor sufficiently resigned. The fact that you do not love him is an unhappiness, a calm grey unhappiness – yes, Annie, an ordinary unhappiness. But think that you might have loved without return, or loved and been deceived ... That is the only great unhappiness, the unhappiness for which one kills, burns, annihilates ... Forgive me, Annie, I was on the point of forgetting that, here, we are only concerned with you . . . A woman in love finds it very hard to conceal her egoism.

'Advise me . . .' you implore. How easy that is! I feel you are ready for all sorts of silly acts – which you will perform quietly, with a gentle obstinacy, with that young girl's grace that gives such hesitance and charm to your gestures, soft, supple Annie.

All the same, I can't very well say to you straight, 'One can't live with a man one doesn't love, it's filthy indecency,' though that opinion does not differ appreciably from what I really think. But I can at least tell you what I did.

Loaded with a great weight of misery and very little luggage, I went back to my native earth. To die there? To recover there? When I went, I had no idea. The heavenly solitude, the pacifying trees, the blue night that was a good counsellor, the peace of wild animals – those were the things that prevented me from doing something irreparable and gently brought me back to that other land I thought I had lost forever – happiness.

My dear Annie, you can always try.

Good-bye. Don't write to me – except to say that the treatment is working. For I shall be too regretful at being unable to suggest another.

I kiss, from the eyelashes to the chin, your whole face that has the tapering shape and almost the exact colour of a ripe filbert. From so far away, kisses lose their poison and, for a minute, I can pursue our dream in the Margravine's garden – without remorse.

Claudine

TEN

CLAUDINE has deceived me. No, that is unjust. Claudine has deceived herself. The 'country cure' is not a panacea. Besides, it is difficult to cure a sick person unless they have faith.

In the first pages of this diary ... (I had to break off here to scold Toby who, with his ears pricked and his eyes starting out of his head, had once again dragged it away by one corner like the corpse of an enemy.) In the first pages of this diary which has no end and no beginning, which is depraved and diffident, vacillating and rebellious just like myself, I read these words: 'the burden of living alone'. Ignorant Annie! What does *that* burden weigh, compared with the chain I have worn, without respite, for four years, and which I must assume again for life? But I do not want to resume it. It is not liberty in itself that I crave for – I need no further proof of that than my feverish need to keep changing my surroundings and the bitter awareness of my own solitude that makes me see it reflected in this lonely landscape of sky and fields and harsh, grey, red-gashed rocks ... Yet to be able to choose one's own misery ... there are certain people for whom that represents their ideal of happiness ...

Alas! I am one of them. I have arrived and already I want to leave. Even though Casamène belongs to me, it is too much associated with my whole life with Alain. There is not a corner of this old-fashioned estate where I could not easily identify traces left by our childhood games; in the romantic shrubbery, under the trees of the 'little forest' – a modest copse which I called by this grandiose name – in the dark gloomy shed where the rusted tools suggest some medieval torture-chamber. Near the ravine, a chestnut-tree still bears the cruel scars of a wire Alain fastened tight round its trunk, maybe twelve years ago; the bark has broken out in a blistered swelling. That was where my stern companion was Snake's-Eye, chief of a tribe of Redskins, and I was his domesticated little squaw who tended the fire of pine-cones. It was one of his favourite games and part of it involved his being extremely severe with me and constantly scolding me.

He has never liked Casamène. My impractical dreamer of a grandfather laid out these few acres in an exaggeratedly picturesque style: a ravine, *wild*, of course; two mounts; a dell; a grotto; a belvedere; a great avenue to give a long vista; exotic shrubs; a paved carriage-drive sufficiently winding to give the impression of traversing miles on his property ... Everything about the place, Alain used to say, was utterly ridiculous. Very likely it is. At this moment all I see in it is the poignant sadness of an abandoned garden. Under this white sun, already as pallid as in October, it has the mournful luxuriance of a cemetery. 'The pacifying trees ! ...' Ah, Claudine, I could sob if I were not so scared, so petrified by loneliness. The unhappy trees here know no peace themselves and can give none to others. Beautiful, twisted oak with the fettered feet, how many years have you stretched your trembling branches up to the sky, like trembling hands ? What straining effort towards freedom bent you under the wind, then forced you upright again so that your limbs are all tortured angles ? All round you, your stunted, deformed, earthbound children are already stretching up beseeching arms.

Other captive creatures, like that silver birch-tree, resign themselves to their fate. So does that delicate larch, but it weeps and shivers under its torrent of silky hair and I can hear its shrill lament from my window as the gusty wind buffets it ... Oh, the sadness of all these tormented trees, tethered fast by their roots! How could any pliant, uncertain spirit ever have looked to them for peace and oblivion? It was not in trees, Claudine, or in frisking animals, it was only in yourself there lay strength and vitality and joy at once dazzling and blinding.

It is raining, which makes everything worse. I have lit the lamp early and shut myself up in my room. I am in a state of acute nervous tension; even the heavy closed shutters and the sound of Léonie having a loud conversation with the gardener's little girl do little to reassure me. The fire crackles – we need fires already – so does the woodwork. When the flame is quiet, the buzzing silence fills my ears. The clawed feet of a rat are distinctly audible running overhead, above the joists of the ceiling, and Toby, my little black guardian, looks up ferociously in the direction of this inaccessible enemy. For heaven's sake, Toby, don't bark! If you bark, the shattered silence will fall in fragments on my head, like the plaster of an old – too old – house ...

It is late, but I dare not go to bed yet. I shall sit up by the dying fire, till the wick of the lamp burns low. I listen to muffled rustlings, to the breath of the wind blowing the leaves along the gravel, to all the footsteps of small, unknown animals. Just now, to give myself courage, I touched the broad blade of a hunting-knife. But the chill feel of the metal, instead of reassuring me, only frightened me more.

What idiotic panic! Don't these friendly pieces of furniture know me any more? Yes, but they know I am going to leave them and they will not shelter me. Old piano with the fluted carving, I wearied you with my scales. 'More energy, my little Annie, more energy!' Even then! This portrait of a wasp-waisted student, copied from a daguerreotype, is my grandfather. He dug wells on the tops of mountains, started an enterprise for cultivating truffles, tried to illuminate the bottom of the sea 'by means of whale-oil burning in transparent vessels, hermetically sealed' (!); in short he light-heartedly ruined his wife and daughter, showed not the slightest remorse, and was adored by both of them. What an elegant waist he had, if the likeness is a true one! A modern woman might envy it. A beautiful, dreamy forehead, the inquisitive eyes of a child, small white-gloved hands – that is all that I know of him.

Above the piano, on the wall, is a bad photograph of my father; I only knew him as old and blind. A distinguished-looking man with white whiskers – how do I come to be the daughter of anyone so ... ordinary?

Of my mother, nothing. Not a single picture, not a single letter. Grandmother Lajarrisse refused even to talk of her to me; all she ever said was: 'Pray for her, my child. Ask God to have mercy on all those who have disappeared, on all exiles, on all the dead ...' Really, it is rather late in the day to begin worrying about my mother! Let her remain for me what I always imagined her; a pretty, unhappy creature who ran away or who killed herself. I feel sorry for her but not really concerned.

Two letters arrived for me this morning – enough to make me doubly uneasy. The huge one, thank heaven, was from Claudine; the other from Alain. I woke up feeling stronger and more alert, soothed by the freshness of the early hour – the cuckoo-clock in the kitchen had just croaked its two notes eight times – by the fragrant

143

tea steaming in my blue cup, by Toby's delirious jumping up and down and whining as he waited hungrily for me to finish my breakfast and give him his. I could breathe a new lightness and excitement in the air, a holiday atmosphere of going away. That is *my* way of enjoying the peace of the country, Claudine – daydreaming to the jingle of harness-bells on the road ... I imagined myself as a young woman of the 1830s. A Creole maybe ? They were in fashion then. An unhappy marriage – an elopement – my flimsy, inappropriate clothes, my ribboned sandals scuffed by the pebbles on the drive – the heavy chaise – the steaming post-horses – what else ? The broken spring, the surprises on the road, the providential encounter ... All the charming, absurd, sentimental romancing of our grandmothers !

In the envelope with the French stamp, there were only a few lines from Claudine.

My dear little Annie,

I do not know where to find you. I only hope this reaches you to tell you that Marthe, who is back in Paris, explains your flight in a few brief words: 'My sister-in-law is having a difficult pregnancy and has gone to the country to rest.' That was the respite I wished for you! Perhaps everything will seem simpler as a result? This is also to tell you that Léon and his wife appear to be in perfect health – and in perfect harmony.

Good-bye, I just wanted to reassure you – and to warn you. Only that ... and to have some news of you for I can't be satisfied with Marthe's explanation. I envisaged you menaced by every kind of danger – barring myself. I said: 'Don't write to me if the remedy fails.' But that only applies to the remedy! I want to know everything about you ... about you whom I have so virtuously renounced. A note, a picture-postcard, a telegram, some sign . . . Make that my reward, Annie. Cured, or ill, or 'lost' as they say, or even – what Marthe says . . . Ugh! no, not that! Remain the slim fragile amphora that two clasped arms can encircle so easily.

Your

Claudine

That was all! Yes, that was all. Even Claudine's tender anxiety did not satisfy me. When, like me, one has nothing in oneself one hopes for everything from another . . .

A weary lassitude had clouded that bright hour. Why did I have to be reminded of those other people and those other days? I re-read Claudine's letter and its tiresome solicitude revived dim, almost effaced pictures in my mind. Through a haze of them I stared at the square envelope addressed in Alain's stiff writing without really seeing it. . . . Dakar, Dakar . . . where had I seen that name inscribed in black in a little circle? Why Dakar? The last time, it was Buenos Aires . . .

With a cry, I emerged from my daze. Dakar! Why, he was coming back, he was on his way, he was getting nearer, he would be here tomorrow, any moment now! So that was what the treacherous calm of this morning had in store, was it? In opening it, my clumsy fingers tore the letter as well as the envelope, the incredibly neat handwriting danced before my eyes . . . I read at random:

'My dear Annie . . . at last . . . return journey . . . met our friends X . . . travelling for pleasure . . . insist on my staying with them . . . matter of ten days . . . find house ready, Annie happy . . .'

Ten days, ten days! Fate had granted me no longer than that to make up my mind. It was not much. But it would be enough.

'Léonie!'

'Madame?'

She was holding three new-born kittens in her apron and explained, laughingly, to excuse herself:

'I was just a-going to drown 'em.'

'Then hurry up and do it. The trunks, the dressing-case – the whole lot strapped up and ready to catch the five o'clock express. We're going back to Paris.'

'What, again!'

'Does that annoy you? I should hate to force you to remain a minute longer in service with someone who goes against your wishes.'

'I didn't say that, Madame . . .'

'Hurry up. Monsieur tells me he will soon be arriving home.'

She went upstairs and I heard her taking her revenge by violently pulling open drawers and slamming the doors of cupboards.

ELEVEN

ALL these parcels, all these cardboard boxes! The room
is permeated with a composite smell of new leather,
black tarred paper, and rough, unworn wool, to which
the big waterproof cape contributes a quota of bitumen.
I have spent my time to some purpose since my hurried
return. I have been incessantly at the bootmaker's, the
tailor's, the hatter's . . . That sounds like a man talking,
not a woman, but fashion is more to blame for that than
I am.

In the five days I have ordered so many, many things
and had them delivered! I have climbed so many stairs,
instructed so many obsequious tradesmen, taken off my
blouse and skirt so many times and felt my bare arms
shiver under the cold fingers of 'head fitters' that my
head is whirling. Never mind, it's worth it. I am slipping
my collar.

At the moment, I am sitting here, slightly dazed, admiring my treasures. Those beautiful big lace-up shoes, flat
and tapered as skiffs on their low English heels! One
ought to be able to tramp steadily for miles on those
little yellow boats. At least, I presume so! My husband
preferred me to wear Louis XV heels – more 'feminine'
. . . Because he preferred them, I don't want any! Neither
would he approve in the least of this rust-coloured coat
and skirt, the colour of a red squirrel's fur, whose trim
skirt flares out so simply and neatly. Personally, I love it.
Its sober, tailored line makes me look slimmer than ever
and its tawny colour emphasizes the blue of my eyes –
exaggerates it so that it positively makes one's mouth
water . . . And those masculine stitched gloves, that

severe felt hat trimmed with an eagle's feather! So many novelties, so many gestures of defiance, go to my head as does the unexpected charm of this hotel bedroom. An eminently respectable hotel . . . two steps from our house – no one would ever guess I was in hiding.

Without bothering about probability, I told Léonie: 'The house needs urgent repairs. Monsieur will join me at the Impérial-Voyage.' Ever since, the poor thing has come round every morning to take orders and to complain.

'Madame, would you believe it? The builder still hasn't come to do those repairs what Madame wrote to him about.'

'It's not possible, Léonie! The only thing is . . . perhaps Monsieur has sent him special instructions?'

And I dismiss her with a smile so benevolent that it intimidates her.

I am feeling tired. While I am waiting for tea-time, I am caressing the finest of my new toys with my eyes – but only with my eyes because I am frightened to touch it. My very latest toy; I only bought it a few minutes ago. It is a dainty, dainty little black revolver that looks like Toby. (Toby, *don't* lick that shiny cardboard, you'll give yourself stomach-ache!) It has two safety-catches, six chambers, a cleaning-rod, all sorts of things. I bought it from Alain's gunsmith. The man who sold it to me carefully explained the mechanism, all the while glancing at me furtively with a fatalistic expression as if he were thinking: 'Another of them! What a tragedy! So young! Still, after all, I've got to sell my knick-knacks . . .'

I feel remarkably well. I am enjoying the kind of rest I have not known for a long time. Someone with quite good taste must have furnished this little yellow drawing-room and the Louis XVI bedroom that opens out of it. Here, my irritable, fastidious instinct does not

suspect dirty carpets or dubious corners in the upholstery. The light falls softly on smooth, polished furniture and matt woodwork painted a restful greyish white.
When I go out, an old gentleman in a morning-coat en-
throned behind the desk, smiles at me as if I were his
daughter ... At night I sleep for hours, on a good plump
firm mattress.

I had gone off into a momentary daydream that I was
a tranquil, middle-aged, dried-up English spinster and
that I was staying as a paying guest with a delightful
French family when suddenly there was a knock at the
door.

'Come in !'

The knock was repeated.

'I said, ''Come in'' ...'

The quaint little chambermaid who looks like a mouse
put her head round the door.

'Is it my tea, Marie ?'

'Yes, Madame, and a visitor for Madame.'

'A visitor !'

I leapt to my feet, still holding my yellow shoes by
their laces. The mouse's face looked scared.

'Why yes, Madame ! It's a lady.'

I trembled all over; there was a buzzing in my ears.

'You're sure it's ... it's a lady ?'

Marie burst out laughing like a stage maid in a
comedy : I could hardly blame her.

'Did you say I was in ? ... Tell her to come up.'

I leant against the table for support, and waited. A
hundred idiotic notions flashed through my mind ... This
lady was Marthe and Alain was with her ... They were
going to take me back ... I stared insanely at the black
toy ...

A footstep brushed the carpet ... Good heavens, it

was Claudine! How pleased, oh how pleased I was to see her!

I threw myself on her neck with such an 'Ah!' of relief that she drew back a little in surprise.

'Annie . . . who were you expecting?'

I pressed her hands, I slipped my arm under hers and pulled her towards the gilded cane sofa with nervous, urgent gestures that she gently repulsed, as if she were uneasy . . .

'Who was I expecting? No one, no one! Oh, I'm so glad it's you!'

Suddenly a suspicion clouded my joy.

'Claudine . . . you haven't been sent? You haven't come on behalf of . . .'

She raised her mobile eyebrows, then frowned impatiently.

'Look here, Annie, we're behaving as if we were acting a scene in a drawing-room comedy . . . you in particular . . . What's happened? And what are you frightened of?'

'Don't be angry, Claudine. It's all so complicated!'

'Do you think so? It's nearly always so simple!'

Meekly, I did not contradict her. She looked pretty, as always, in her own way; her face mysteriously shadowed by a black hat wreathed with blue and white thistles under which I could only make out her eyes, her curly hair, and her ironical, pointed chin . . .

'I'd like to tell you everything, Claudine . . . But, first of all, how did you know I was here?'

She raised her forefinger.

'Shh! . . . Once again you must thank Chance – Chance with a capital C, Annie – which is my servant when it isn't my master . . . It led me to the Louvre – the shop not the gallery – which is one of its temples, then under the arcade of the Théâtre-Français, not far from a famous gunsmith's where a slim little creature with burning blue eyes was buying . . .'

'Ah ! So that was why . . .'

So she had been frightened too . . . She had supposed . . . It was kind but a little naïve. I smiled surreptitiously.

'What, you mean you thought . . . No, no Claudine, don't be alarmed ! People don't do it just like that, for no definite reason . . .'

'Blow their brains out ? . . . I fear your argument doesn't convince me. On the contrary, nine times out of ten, it *is* for no definite reason . . .'

She was making fun of me, but all my heart was swelling with gratitude to her. Not for her slightly melodramatic apprehensions just now but because in her, and only in her, I had met with pity, loyalty, affection that had blazed for a moment into passion . . . everything life had denied me.

Her speech was harsh, but her eyes were tender. There was anxiety behind the raillery. She was not quite sure what she ought to prescribe for me. She was an ignorant, intelligent, superstitious little doctor, an osteopath with a touch of divination but lacking in experience . . . I could sense all this but took care not to tell her so. It was too late to change my habits.

'This place might be a lot worse,' observed Claudine, looking about her. 'This little drawing-room is rather charming.'

'Yes, isn't it ? And the bedroom – look . . . You wouldn't think you were in a hotel.'

'You most certainly wouldn't. It's much more like a delicious little flat people hire for assignations.'

'Is it ? I don't know anything about those.'

'Neither do I, Annie,' she laughed. 'But I've had them described to me.'

This revelation left me brooding. 'A flat people hired for assignations ...' It was an ironical suggestion to make to a woman who was expecting no one!

'Have some tea, Claudine.'

'Ugh! How strong it is! Lots of sugar, for goodness' sake. Ah, here's Toby! Come here, Toby, you charming black angel, you square frog, you noble-browed thinker, you sausage on four paws! What an extraordinary mug you've got – like a sentimental murderer – my darling, my precious! ...'

All at once, she had become completely Claudine again. Her hat had fallen off and she was on all fours on the carpet, hugging the little dog with all her might. Toby, who bares his strong, uneven teeth menacingly at everyone, was completely bewitched and let her roll him about like a ball ...

'Is Fanchette well?'

'Very well thank you. Believe it or not, she's had another three children. That makes nine this year. I shall write to a birth-control specialist. Most shaming children, moreover – greyish, badly marked ... their father must have been the coal-man or the laundryman ... But who cares? it does her good.'

She drank her cup of tea with both hands, like a little girl. That was how she had held my head tilted back for a minute, for just one minute, in the Margravine's garden ...

'Claudine ...'

'What?'

'Nothing ...'

'Nothing what, Annie?'

'Nothing ... new. It's for you to question me.'

Her eyes changed back from those of a mischievous schoolgirl into a woman's eyes, sombre and penetrating.

'May I ? With no subject barred ? . . . Good ! Has your husband come back ?'

Sitting beside her, I lowered my eyes on my folded hands as if I were in the confessional.

'No.'

'Is he coming back soon ?'

'In four days' time.'

'What have you decided ?'

I admitted, under my breath :

'Nothing ! Nothing !'

'Then what's all this equipment ?'

With her chin, she indicated the trunk, the clothes, the cardboard boxes strewn everywhere . . .

'Just some odds and ends for the autumn season.'

'Hmm. I see.'

She scrutinized my face suspiciously . . . I could not stand it any longer. Let her blame me, if she liked, but I could not bear her to imagine some sordid escapade, some kind of ridiculous elopement. Hurriedly, with the words tumbling over each other, I brought out a wildly disjointed story.

'Listen . . . Marthe told me that Alain . . . with Valentine Chessenet . . .'

'Oh ! the bitch !'

'So I came back to Paris . . . I . . . I nearly demolished Alain's desk . . . I found the letters.'

'Excellent !'

Claudine's eyes were sparkling and she was twisting a handkerchief. Encouraged, I became feverishly worked up.

'. . . And then I left everything on the floor, letters, papers – everything . . . he'll find them, he'll know it was me . . . Only I can't stand any more, I can't stand any more, do you realize ? I don't love him enough to stay with him. I want to get away, get away, get away . . .'

Choking with tears and my spate of words, I raised my head to get a gulp of breath. Claudine delicately stroked both my hands and asked very gently:

'So . . . you want to get a divorce?'

I stared at her, dumbfounded.

'A divorce . . . whatever for?'

'Really! You are the most extraordinary girl! Why, because you don't want to live with him any more!'

'I most certainly don't. But is it necessary to have a divorce?'

'Well, it's still the surest, if not the shortest method. What a babe-in-arms you are!'

I had not the heart to laugh. I was beginning to panic.

'But do you realize I don't want to see him again! I'm frightened!'

'Bravely said. Frightened of what?'

'Of him . . . that he'll make me go back . . . that he'll talk me round . . . I'm frightened of seeing him . . . Perhaps he'll be very nasty . . .'

I shuddered.

'You poor little thing!' Claudine murmured very low, without looking at me.

She seemed to be thinking very hard.

'What do you advise me to do, Claudine?'

'It's difficult. I'm not all sure, myself. We must ask Renaud.'

Terrified, I cried:

'No! Nobody . . . Nobody!'

'You're very unreasonable, child. Wait a minute . . . Did you take the lady's letters?' she asked me suddenly.

'No,' I admitted, slightly taken aback. 'What for? They don't belong to me!'

'Of all the reasons!' exclaimed Claudine very contemptuously, with a shrug. 'Hell . . . I can't think of anything. Have you any money?'

'Yes ... Very nearly eight thousand francs. Alain left me a lot when he went away.'

'I'm not asking about that ... Money of your own – any private means?'

'Wait ... there's three hundred thousand francs of my dowry ... And then there's the fifty thousand francs in cash Grandmother Lajarrisse left me three years ago.'

'That's fine, you won't die of starvation. Looking ahead, would it worry you if *he* divorced you?'

I replied with a haughty gesture.

'Nor me either,' said Claudine quaintly. 'Well then, my dear child ... go.'

I did not stir: I did not say a word.

'My opinion and my prescription don't produce loud cries of enthusiasm, Annie? I can understand that. But I've come to the end of my tether and my genius.'

I raised my eyes and looked at her through a mist of fresh tears. Without speaking, I indicated the trunk, the tough clothes, the long shoes, the waterproof cape ... all that puerile globe-trotter's gear I had bought in these last few days. She smiled and her piercing gaze softened.

'Yes, I see, I see. I saw at once. Where are you going, my Annie, whom I'm going to lose?'

'I don't know.'

'Is that true?'

'I swear it.'

'Good-bye, Annie.'

'Good-bye ... Claudine.'

I implored her, huddled close against her:

'Tell me again ...'

'What, darling?'

'That Alain can't hurt me if he catches me up?'

'He won't catch you up. At least, not at once. Before you see him, you'll see various unpleasant people who'll fiddle about with papers, then will come the divorce, the blame laid on Annie – and freedom.'

'Freedom.' (I spoke almost in a whisper, as she had.) 'Is it a very heavy burden, Claudine? Is it very difficult to manage? Or will it be a great joy – the cage open – all the world before me?'

She answered very low, shaking her curly head:

'No, Annie, not all at once ... Perhaps never ... You'll carry the marks of the chain for a long time. Perhaps, too, there are people who are born submissive? ... But there's something worse than that ... I'm afraid for you ...'

'Whatever of?'

She looked me in the face. I saw Claudine's eyes and Claudine's tears shining in all their beauty – small tears that did not fall, golden eyes that had refused me their light ...

'I'm afraid of the Meeting. You will meet him, the man who has not yet crossed your path. Yes, yes,' she insisted as I made a gesture of violent dissent, 'that man is waiting for you somewhere. It's right, it's inevitable. Only Annie, my dear Annie, do you know how to recognize him, don't be deceived, because there are doubles, there are any number of shadows who simulate him, there are caricatures of him. Between you and him there are all the ones you have to step over or push aside ...'

'Claudine – suppose I got old before I met him?'

She raised her graceful arm in a gesture that transcended herself:

'Still keep going on! He is waiting for you on the other side of life.'

I was silent out of respect for this faith in love. I was a little proud, too, of being the only person ... or almost the only one ... to know the true Claudine, exalted and fierce as a young druidess.

Just as in Bayreuth, I was ready to do her will, good or evil. She gazed at me with those eyes in which I wanted to see the light that had dazzled me in the Margravine's garden . . .

'Yes, Annie, wait. Perhaps there isn't a man who deserves . . . all this.'

Her hand lightly brushed and caressed my shoulders. I leant towards her and she saw in my face my offering of my whole self, my utter abandonment, the very words I was going to say . . . Quickly she put her warm hand over my mouth, then raised it to her lips and kissed it.

'Good-bye, Annie.'

'Claudine . . . one second . . . only one second ! I want . . . I want you to love me from a distance – you who could have loved me – you who are staying here.'

'I'm not staying, Annie. I've already gone. Can't you feel that ? I've left everything . . . except Renaud . . . for Renaud. Friends are traitors, books are deceivers. Paris will see no more of Claudine. She will grow old among her relatives the trees, with her lover and friend. He will grow old more quickly than I shall, but solitude can work miracles. Perhaps I can give a little of my own life to prolong his.'

She had opened the door, and I was going to lose my only friend . . . What gesture, what word would retain her ? Ought I not to have . . . ? But already the white door had hidden her dark slenderness and I could hear the light rustle of footsteps, that had announced her arrival, dying away . . . Claudine had gone !

I have just read Alain's telegram. In thirty-six hours he will be here, and I . . . Tonight I am catching the Paris–Carlsbad express on which we travelled only last month to Bayreuth. From there, I do not know yet. Alain does not speak German — that puts another little obstacle between us.

Since the day before yesterday, I have done so much thinking that my head is exhausted. My maid is going to be as astonished as my husband. I am only taking my two little black friends, Toby the dog and Toby the revolver . . . I shall be a very well-protected woman, shall I not ? I am going away resolutely, not hiding my tracks, but not marking them with little pebbles either . . . This escape of mine is not a crazy flight on the spur of the moment. For four months I have been slowly gnawing away at my rope till it has finally frayed and parted. All that was needed was simply that the gaoler should carelessly leave the prisoner unguarded. Once his back was turned, she became aware both of the horror of the prison and of light shining through the chinks of the door.

Before me lies the troubled future. Let me know nothing of tomorrow, let no presentiment warn me of what is in store — Claudine has told me too much already ! I want to hope and to fear that there are countries where everything is new, unknown cities whose only lure is their name, skies under which an alien soul replaces your own . . . Somewhere in the whole wide world, shall I not find the nearest thing to paradise for a little creature like me ?

Standing in front of the glass, dressed all in tawny frieze, I have just said good-bye to the Annie who once lived here. Good-bye, Annie ! Feeble and vacillating as you are, I love you. Alas, I have no one but you to love.

I am resigned to whatever may come. Just for a passing moment, I can foresee with sad clairvoyance what this new life of mine will be like. I shall be the woman travelling alone who intrigues a hotel dining-room for a week, with whom schoolboys on holiday and arthritics in spas suddenly fall violently in love ... I shall be the solitary diner, whose pallor provides scandal with an excuse for inventing all kinds of drama ... the lady in black, or the lady in blue, whose melancholy reserve frustrates and repulses the compatriot she meets on her travels ... Also the one whom a man remorselessly pursues because she is pretty and a stranger, or because of the big, lustrous pearls he has noticed on her fingers ... The one who is murdered one night in a hotel bedroom and whose body is found outraged and bleeding ...

No, Claudine, I do not shudder. All that is life, time flowing on, the hoped-for miracle that may lie round the next bend of the road. It is because of my faith in that miracle that I am escaping.

COLETTE

'I know of few works which have today offered me such an amused and perfect joy' – *André Gide*

'There is nothing to explain, nothing to criticize, one has only to admire' – *Henri de Montherlant*

Claudine at School

The intimate secrets of a sixteen-year-old make a novel which is more daring than *Bonjour Tristesse*, more scandalous than *Lolita*.

Claudine in Paris

At seventeen Claudine begins to explore Paris and its vices, and gets more and more involved with a remote cousin old enough to be her father.

Claudine Married

The story of a young married woman's Lesbian affair, encouraged by her husband.

Other titles by Colette:

THE CAPTIVE
THE PURE AND THE IMPURE
MY APPRENTICESHIP *and* MUSIC-HALL SIDELIGHTS